A RUN FOR
THE MONEY

Other books by Gina Ardito:

The Bonds of Matri-money

A RUN FOR THE MONEY

•

Gina Ardito

AVALON BOOKS

NEW YORK

Published by Thomas Bouregy & Co., Inc.
160 Madison Avenue, New York, NY 10016

Library of Congress Cataloging-in-Publication Data

Ardito, Gina.
    A run for the money / Gina Ardito.
        p. cm.
    ISBN 978-0-8034-9965-2 (hardcover : acid-free paper)
    1. Treasure hunt (game)—Fiction.   2. Inheritance and
succession—Fiction.   I. Title.

    PS3601.R43R86 2009
    813'.6—dc22   2009004069

PRINTED IN THE UNITED STATES OF AMERICA
ON ACID-FREE PAPER
BY HADDON CRAFTSMEN, BLOOMSBURG, PENNSYLVANIA

For Barbara, the sister of my heart.
Thank you for sharing the special moments
that make up the memories of your life.
In you I found not only family, but a dear friend.

Chapter One

When Nicole Fleming squirmed, the sound of sweaty thighs unsticking from her leather chair resonated like a blaring trumpet. Inside the conference room for the law offices of Stern, Stern & Weitzman, two pairs of male eyes mirrored disgust. Oh, God, how embarrassing. Why hadn't she worn pantyhose today?

Because encasing legs in nylon during Manhattan's dog days of July better suited a game-show challenge than a will reading. Between the hellish temperatures in subway tunnels and the swelter rising up from city asphalt street-side, an extra layer of clothing would have wilted her long before she reached the mausoleum lobby.

Fresh heat rocketed up her cheeks. Muttering a low "Sorry" to the staring gentlemen, she averted her gaze to the wall of leather-bound books on her right. Their red and green spines,

1

embossed with gold lettering, were at least two inches thick. Had the attorney really read all those books? Who had that much free time?

Not her. She barely finished one month's *Cosmo* before the next issue landed in her mailbox.

At the head of the long mahogany table, Andrew Stern, Esq., cleared his throat and shuffled a sheaf of papers atop a manila folder. "If I may continue . . . ?"

Nodding, Nicole straightened. The man seated across from her stared with the intensity of a buzzard on a dying gazelle. Who was this guy? And why were there just the two of them in this room with the attorney? Papa Joe had dozens of friends, and, if memory served, a daughter with a family of her own. So how come she was stuck with Mr. Monogrammed Shirtsleeves and the unblinking vulture of doom? Where were the truly grieving? Those who'd loved Papa Joe the way she had?

"There are, of course," Mr. Stern said, lifting a longer sheet from the pile of standard-sized papers, "a few charitable donations and family obligations. But the bulk of Mr. Corbet's estate will fall to the two of you, depending upon your adherence with his final wishes."

Nicole sniffed. Some estate. As far as she knew, Papa Joe's only worldly possession was a mangled mass of chrome, once a primo 1980 Harley Davidson Roadster. At least until a tractor trailer had made an illegal U-turn, destroying both ride and rider.

Tears pricked her eyelids. Never again would she hear his folksy voice, spouting the wisdom of the ages. His chipped-front-tooth smile would never flash in welcome. She'd never again smell his unique scent of motor oil and Old Spice in her kitchen.

"Exactly how much money are we talking about?" the vulture asked.

His callousness transformed Nicole's grief to smoldering anger. "Wow." She forced a light air far from the turmoil churning her gut. "Did you leave your membership card at the door?"

Dark eyes flashed like the silver wrapper on a semi-sweet chocolate bar. "What membership card?"

"The one that verifies you're human." When he continued to stare blankly, she added, "You know. A guy with a working heart."

With the speed of a snapped cable, his jaw dropped. Good. In the few minutes she'd spent with him there, she'd picked up his vibe. Few people dared challenge him.

Correction. Few *women* dared challenge him. No wonder, really. Whoever he was, this man had the sultry look of palm trees in sunset, drinks with teeny umbrellas, and warm Caribbean water kissing bare flesh. Under normal circumstances, she might have found the whole Fantasy Island package a turn-on. But Papa Joe's sudden death had encased her in dry ice.

Eyes narrowing to cobra slits, the man whirled to the attorney at the head of the table. "Who *is* this woman?"

Mr. Stern blinked several times. Finally, he cocked his head. "Mr. LaPalma, this is Ms. Fleming. Nicole Fleming. Your grandfather's stepdaughter."

As if swerving to avoid an oncoming truck, Mr. LaPalma suddenly rolled back his chair. "*She's* the succubus' daughter?"

Fine hairs danced on Nicole's nape. "Could you control the urge to talk about me like I'm the senile auntie in the corner? If you want to know about me, Mr. LaPalma, why not ask me?"

A smile, filled with the same snakelike malice as his eyes, bloomed over his face. "Yup. You're the succubus' daughter, all right."

Any response she made now would only cause delight. So she ignored him. Not because of some perceived insult at his calling her mother a succubus. After all, Papa Joe had assigned that particular term of endearment to his ex-wife years ago.

No. Having this stranger draw a link between her and Ice Princess Rhoda stung. Okay, so maybe she should have expected a rude retort after her crack about him not being human. But his barb had struck extra-tender flesh. Hands folded in her lap, she settled her gaze on Mr. Stern's disapproving frown.

"I'd advise you two to put aside whatever petty differences you harbor," the attorney said. "Your tasks will be inordinately easier if you get along."

"T-tasks? What tasks?" An anxiety train barreled through her veins, sparking jitters in her blood.

With an exaggerated sigh, Mr. Stern removed his wire-rimmed glasses and rubbed his eyes. "Perhaps we should move on to the video." Swerving in his swivel chair, he punched a button on a control panel on the wall behind him.

Pop! Blackout shades flipped into place inside the windows, blocking light from filtering in around them. A low click pierced the quiet room. Before Nicole could become fully accustomed to the darkness, the flat-screen television, mounted on the wall on her left, burst to life. The room glowed with staticky white light until, on screen, a wrinkled face topped with sparse, snowy hair, appeared. She flinched.

How could Papa Joe be right there, in living color, almost close enough to touch, yet still be gone?

For a long moment, the old man's gaze remained fixed offstage. Finally, he mouthed the word, "Now?" then cleared his throat and faced the camera directly. "Well, well. Look who's here. My two favorite people in the whole world." When he grinned, the creases around his eyes deepened to gullies. "Hello, Nicole. How's it going, Dante? If you're watching this, it means two things. First, I've gone from this life."

Renewed tears pricked Nicole's eyes.

But Papa Joe's folksy voice chastised from beyond the grave. "Now, no crying, Nicole, honey. We can't control our fates. I only hope I went out in a blaze of glory, like Butch and Sundance. I hope my chute didn't open or I got trampled by the bulls in Pamplona." Hands clasped in prayer, he turned his gaze toward the ceiling. "Please, God, don't let me have slipped in the bathtub."

Despite her grief, Nicole smiled. *Yes, Papa Joe. You got your wish. Macho to the end . . .*

"The second thing you two have in common," the old man continued, "is that each of you has a bitter, greedy woman wringing you dry."

Nape hairs prickled anew, and she turned to discover Mr. LaPalma's eyes boring into her again. Hadn't anyone ever taught him manners? No problem. She knew exactly how to deal with rudeness.

"Something wrong?" Leaning her upper body across the gleaming tabletop, she bared her teeth. "Do I have a poppy seed stuck in my gums?"

As she expected, he didn't answer, but refocused his attention on the television. Flashing him a look of triumph, she resettled in her chair.

"Nicole," Papa Joe's image said. "You've got the succubus. Now, I want you to know, I had nothing to do with the bargain she struck with you. Emotional blackmail, plain and simple. But you know Rhoda. One for all and all for Rhoda."

Unfortunately, yes. Nicole knew her mother all too well. And once again, Papa Joe had summed her up with one droll remark.

"Dante," Papa Joe said, "you're still trying to get your ex-wife off the payroll. I warned you against marrying that she-devil, told you she'd leave you bleeding in the end. But you were in loooooovvvvve." He drew the last word out with enough acid to etch glass.

From the corner of her eye, Nicole watched Mr. LaPalma—Dante—squirm. Since he wore slacks, expensive summer-weight wool if her shopper's eyes guessed correctly, no embarrassing sounds emitted. Still, the action itself, and the pained look on his face, suggested he'd sunk to a new level of discomfort.

So maybe Dante LaPalma wasn't the arrogant vulture she'd first thought. Maybe he was like her, desperate and running out of time. According to Papa Joe, they had a lot in common. And she'd always trusted Papa Joe's judgment.

"Now, I know what you two are thinking," he said. " 'Get to the point, old man.' So, here you go. Nicole, take a good look at Dante."

When she turned her full focus on him, he shifted in the chair and glanced away. Dark pink color stained his throat.

Turnabout is fair play, Dante LaPalma . . .

"Handsome devil, isn't he?" Papa Joe prompted.

A diabolical joke flew into her head. Her gaze still pinning LaPalma, she flipped her hand to and fro. "Eh."

LaPalma glowered, and she stifled the giggle rising in her throat.

"Looks a little like I did at his age," Papa Joe continued, "but he's also got some of his father's Latin DNA too. Now, despite his name, which probably has you thinking about the circles of hell, Dante's more than eye candy. He's a good man, trustworthy, dependable, the only one in my family worth a darn."

Her chocoholic soul could definitely appreciate the eye candy bit. In fact, this guy's looks were so sweet they could give her cavities. Rich cocoa eyes set in a caramel-golden face, sculpted cheekbones with the merest hint of stubble. He wore a hunter green polo shirt that clung to broad shoulders and well-developed biceps.

"Dante," Papa Joe said, "I want you to look at Nicole. *Really* look at her, not like she's the enemy simply 'cuz she's a female. Pretty as a summer's day, ain't she? And, like you, she's trustworthy and dependable. As different from the succubus as kittens are from snakes."

He barely glanced at her.

What the . . . ?

Ten minutes ago, he couldn't take his eyes off her. Now, when Papa Joe told him to look at her, to really look at her, he gave her the cursory once-over.

"Already got me burned into your memory, huh?" Her grin so wide her cheeks stretched, she turned her attention back to Papa Joe on the high-definition television screen.

"Now, what I'm about to tell you two is for your ears only. Well . . . yours and that shark, Andrew's." His voice lowered to a gravelly whisper. "I've got a special codicil set up for you two. Most of my will encompasses the rest of the family. Believe me, I've provided them all with enough money to prevent any grousing that they got short shrift. I know if that former wife of Dante's finds out about the codicil, she'll manipulate his affection for Gitan until she gets what she thinks she's owed. And softhearted dunce you can be, Dante, you'll give in to her for the boy's sake."

Dante snorted, but said nothing.

"Rhoda, of course, would find a way to make life so miserable for you, Nicole, you'd turn over every dime and then some to shut her up."

Nicole gasped. "I would not!"

As if he'd heard her denial, Papa Joe shook his head like one of those bobble toys. "Fear not. Andrew and I set up my estate to make such an occurrence impossible. If Dante or Nicole declines any portion of his or her share, the entire inheritance goes to charity. Including the money I set aside for the rest of the family. Even that grasping ex Linda's smart enough to know a little piece of pie is better than none at all. And Rhoda, as per our divorce settlement, will receive nothing. Once the ink dried our signatures on that nasty court document, she ceased to deserve anything from me. I wouldn't spit on her if she were on fire." He shivered dramatically, and then rubbed his hands together. "So . . . I'll bet you're wondering, what is this inheritance?"

He paused, and the room grew so still, Nicole swore she'd stopped breathing. In fact, the only sound inside the attorney's office was the *tick-tick-tick* of the mahogany and brass grandfather clock.

After several heart-thudding seconds, Papa Joe expelled air through his chapped lips. Chair squeaking under the shift in his weight, he leaned closer from the giant screen. "It's a great treasure, kids," he said in a hushed tone. "The greatest treasure in all the world. And you two alone are fortunate enough to be given a chance to possess it. But like all great treasures, this one's not out in the open or stashed in some bank vault."

Huh? Nicole stole a glance at Dante. Did he understand what Papa Joe was talking about? Judging by the quirk to his lips and his puckered brow, she assumed the answer was a big fat nope.

"Ever see that television show where people race around the world to find a million dollars?" Papa Joe asked. "Well, this is kinda like that. You're going to have to hunt for the treasure. Together. If you cooperate, learn to trust each other, I promise you an adventure the likes of which you've never known. Dive into this headfirst and learn to fly! Where should you start? Put your heads together. Talk to each other about me, share some memories. Cry a little, laugh a lot, and who knows? You might find something valuable. Wherever I am, up or down, I'll be watching and cheering you on. One last thing, kids. I love you both. Always have, always will."

With a static hiss, the screen went snowy.

Andrew Stern, Esq., reached across his desk and pushed the button on his console. The blackout shades disappeared, and white-hot sunlight streamed into the room.

While Nicole blinked her vision back into focus, Mr. Stern's business tone asked, "Any questions?"

Questions? Yeah, Dante had a dozen questions he'd like to ask Mr. Stern.

What was this treasure Gramps talked about? How could he find it? And most important of all, why did he have to team up with *Nicole Fleming* to gain his inheritance?

He still couldn't believe she sat here with him. The succubus' daughter, Nicole Fleming, who could do no wrong in Gramps' eyes.

Funny. She didn't look like much. Oh, she was pretty. Lush blond hair, big blue eyes, and from what he could see, a figure with lots of curves in all the right places. Which only gave Dante another reason to dislike her. After years of listening to Gramps wax poetic about her, Dante was disappointed to discover Nicole was just another pretty woman.

His ex-wife, Linda, was a pretty woman too. Marital experience had taught him pretty women didn't care about anyone but themselves. Linda always expected men to drop everything because she batted her eyelashes and maybe produced a tear or two.

And pretty as she was, Nicole Fleming would no doubt prove to be as difficult as Linda. A sour taste filled his mouth as he studied her through half-mast lids. She'd obviously taken great pains with her appearance for today's meeting. Her purple sandals perfectly matched her skirt. Her hair fell in perfect waves to her shoulders.

An eerie dread sent his stomach pitching. Whatever Gramps had hidden at the end of this yellow brick road better be worth the torture he'd have to endure with Nicole Fleming along for the ride.

"Wait!" She leaned toward the attorney, a frown twisting her pretty pink lips. "I don't understand. What exactly are we looking for?"

"That," the lawyer replied, "I can't tell you."

"Well, you have to tell us something," she pressed. "How much is this treasure worth? What does it look like? Where should we start the search? If we don't know what we're after, how will we know when we've found it?"

"I'm afraid I can't tell you any more regarding the particulars of the treasure."

Dante narrowed his eyes. "Exactly what else *can* you tell us?"

"That it would behoove you two to begin your search immediately," the lawyer replied. "You have several tasks to undertake. Each one will lead to another clue. But your time is not unlimited. Nine months from today, you and Ms. Fleming are expected to return to this office to report on your progress.

Together. If you have discovered the treasure, it is yours to keep for the rest of your lives. If not . . ." Shrugging nonchalantly, he let the sentence trail off.

If not, one person could go after it himself, without having to share a dime with a virtual stranger.

Dante's conscience went from sixty to zero with a *splat*. What was he thinking? Linda's betrayal might have made him desperate, but not dishonest.

Still . . .

What, if anything, prevented either of them from pursuing this so-called treasure on their own when the time limit passed? Had Nicole considered that option? He stole another glance in her direction, but found her expression inscrutable. Well, he'd have plenty of time to discern her motives over the next nine months.

Nine months. What ghastly purgatory had Gramps planned for them that would take nine months?

The lawyer rose, flipping the manila folder closed. "If there are no more questions—"

"Wait!" Nicole repeated. "What's your rush?"

With one extended index finger, Mr. Stern slid his glasses up higher on his nose. "I do have other clients."

"Tough ta-tas." She said the phrase with a smile, yet the undercurrent was undeniably angry.

Dante bit back a smile. So Little Miss Fleming had a temper. Who would have guessed? Certainly not Gramps, who only spoke of his stepdaughter in the most glowing terms. So much for the old man's opinion that she was as different from her mother as a snake from kittens. The only thing kittenish about her was the possibility he might see some fur fly before this meeting ended.

The lawyer offered her the same bland expression he'd worn since they entered the office. "I've already told you all there is to know. The rest is up to the two of you. Now, if you'll excuse me . . ."

Craning her neck, she fixed a glazed stare on the lawyer's backside and swayed her legs in an aggressive rhythm: back, forward, back, forward, building speed, back . . .

The rapid motion drew Dante's attention to something he hadn't noticed in his earlier studies of Nicole Fleming: an imperfection that confused and intrigued him. On the strap of her purple sandal, a quarter-inch square of tan caught his eye. A Band-Aid. Did her shoe have a boo-boo? Or was she so totally clueless she didn't know how to put a Band-Aid adhesive side down on her skin?

"I'm picking up a good backswing here," she hinted, her legs rocking at an almost furious pace.

The attorney's face flushed crimson. "Young lady, if you think you can intimidate me—"

"Ms. Fleming," Dante cut in before the temperature in the room grew from heated to violent. "Why don't you and I grab some lunch somewhere? We may as well get started on this adventure."

She veered toward him so quickly he thought she might kick him instead of the attorney. For a brief moment, her eyes flared the blue fire of a gas stove. Then, with a deep sigh signaling surrender, she let loose with Linda's favorite F word.

"Fine!"

Chapter Two

Despite his death, Papa Joe still had a few tricks up his sleeve. Thus, when Nicole followed Dante out of the attorney's office a few minutes later, each of them clutched a personal letter from the old man.

Nicole's fingers itched to rip the seal and pull out whatever lay inside the envelope. But she and Dante had promised the attorney they'd sit down somewhere quiet and go over the two documents together.

And though Dante might have invited her to join him for lunch, his speedy pace left no doubt he couldn't wait to escape that office and her. Thank God she'd opted for flat sandals rather than heels or she never could've kept up.

As if Moses had parted them, the elevator doors slid open on a *ding* before Dante even had to push the Down button. Half a dozen women, suited in pinstripe gray and black suits exited past him, barreling toward her like the New York Giants' offensive line.

He stepped into the car without breaking stride.

With a shoulder shuffle here and a sidestep there, she managed to maneuver around the blitz only to see the elevator doors begin to slide shut. "Hey!"

Dante shot out a hand to hold the door until she scrambled into the conveyance and stood beside him. "Thanks."

"Uh-huh."

If those two syllables were his idea of friendly conversation, the next nine months would be torturous. In the awkward silence, she stared at the glowing green numbers on the panel above her, watching them descend from ten to L.

Paint dried faster.

Meanwhile, Dante stood far behind her, his back almost touching the wall. Maybe he thought she had cooties.

Yessiree, Papa Joe had set her up for one great big party. Still, what choice did she have? In a few months' time, without this treasure, she'd lose the only home she'd ever known. *Happy thirtieth birthday, Nicole, darling. Get out and stay out.*

Thanks, Mom. Nothing like the devil you know to make the devil you don't more appealing.

The Village Inn sat in the middle of town, a hard-to-miss landmark since the exterior was shaped like a ship's prow, complete with figurehead. The interior, however, more closely resembled a solarium with floor-to-ceiling windows overlooking the Long Island Sound, lush greenery, and cozy white furnishings.

No surprise Nicole chose this particular eatery for their lunchtime strategy session. She needed a little home-field advantage with this guy.

"Nice place," Dante said, glancing around the well-lit dining room.

"It's my favorite restaurant," she admitted. "Not only for the food, but for the scenery as well."

Her gaze wandered to the window where a ferry glided across the placid gray surface of the Sound. Three hundred sixty-five days a year, every hour on the hour, one of the fleet of large white ships transported passengers and cars between Long Island and Connecticut. An antiquated way to travel in this day and age, but residents on both coasts had waged wars to prevent the building of a bridge that might add more traffic, more pollution, and more craziness to already hectic lives.

When she returned her attention to Dante, she saw his dark head buried in the leather-bound menu. Taking advantage of his distraction, she studied the gifts some generous god had bequeathed to this man. Thick dark hair. Broad shoulders, wide as Wyoming. Upper arms thicker than her thighs. Hands with long, slender fingers that looked capable of both crushing a can with ferocity and caressing a curve with finesse. She shivered at the imagined sensation of those fingers stroking her face, the juncture of her neck and shoulder, her hip . . .

God, where was their busboy? She needed ice water—fast. Spotting him in the corner, she tapped a fingernail on her empty glass meaningfully. With a quick nod, he grabbed the silver carafe and headed toward their table. He filled her glass, handed it to her, and she drained it before he finished filling Dante's. With a secretive smile, he filled her glass again, but she refused to lift it while he watched. Only when he'd turned his back did she drain the water a second time.

Her parched throat eased, she addressed Dante as if they were prisoners sharing a cell. "So, what are *you* in for?"

"Hmmm?" He glanced up from the menu, curiosity bubbling in his eyes.

Good Lord, every inch of this man reminded her of a Snickers bar. If she didn't indulge her chocolate addiction soon, she'd wind up licking Dante's fingers before the day ended. Maybe she'd forget her diet and order a chocolate bag for dessert. If she split it with Dante and skipped dinner tonight—and breakfast tomorrow—she'd probably atone for half the calories in the rich, sweet treat. Oh, the heck with it. She'd order the dessert and still eat breakfast tomorrow. She had enough to worry about without sweating a few thousand calories. Which brought her back to her question for Dante . . .

"Papa Joe said we were in similar predicaments," she reminded him. "What's your problem?"

He blinked then jerked his head at her. "You go first. What's *your* problem?"

"What else?" She shrugged, hoping the action came off as nonchalance and not as a way to evade the shivers that racked her at the thought of her pending eviction. "My mother."

"Ah," he said, leaning back and setting the menu on top of his bread plate. "I've heard about her. My condolences."

She smirked at him. "Thanks. I take it your problems have something to do with your wife."

"Ex-wife," he corrected with a grimace.

"Ah."

Before she could press him any further, the waiter appeared to take their orders. She chose her usual chicken pecan salad and the unusual but decadent chocolate bag for dessert.

"We'll split that," she told Dante.

"A chocolate bag?" His eyes widened to horrified saucers. "Sounds ominous."

She snorted a laugh. Ominous? That delicate, bag-shaped shell of dark chocolate stuffed with all sorts of delectable sweets? Ha. The only danger was to a person's waistline.

"Trust me," she said with a dreamy sigh. "You're gonna love it."

His lips quirked in a cockeyed smile. "If you say so." Turning to the waiter, he ordered a rib-eye steak, rare, with a baked potato and sour cream.

The waiter nodded. "Very good, sir, miss."

He scooped the menus off the table and turned around, taking Nicole's napkin with him. Two steps later, the white square fluttered to the floor, unnoticed by the waiter.

She started to get up, but Dante stopped her with a touch of his hand on her wrist.

"Allow me."

"Thanks."

He left his seat and retrieved the napkin, presenting Nicole a new angle to check him out, but her interest disintegrated under his next question. "Okay, I gotta ask. What's with the Band-Aid on your sandal?"

With a grin, she flexed her leg at him. "I broke the strap. But they're my favorite shoes, so I—"

"So you hold them together with a Band-Aid," he finished for her. Then he did a doubletake. "Is that a tattoo on your ankle?"

Pride bubbled up as she cast a glance at the indelible design etched on her ankle. A baseball, complete with red stitching and script, the logo signature for the New York Yankees, branded her skin for eternity. "Yup. Like it?"

His eyebrows rose in twin arcs. "You know, I've seen a lot of tattoos in my time. Until today, I would have sworn that women gravitated toward feminine ideals: butterflies, hearts, flowers. But yours . . . well, let's just say it's unique. You must be very proud."

Sarcasm dripped from his tone, and she narrowed her eyes. "Don't tell me you're a Red Sox fan."

"I'm not a baseball fan at all."

He couldn't have surprised her more if he'd said he wasn't a fan of a cure for cancer. "You're not?"

"Sorry." He shrugged. "I guess I never understood the appeal. A lot of standing around, very little action."

"You obviously don't grasp the subtle nuances, the strategies involved."

"Maybe." Frowning, he touched his fingers to his chin as if seriously considering her argument. "Or maybe I have attention deficit disorder. Where do you stand on football?"

"I never understood the appeal," she tossed back at him. "Grown men killing each other for a triangular ball."

"Oh, well, you just don't understand the subtle nuances, the strategies involved."

"Hmmm . . ." She imitated his pose perfectly, fingers poised on chin, mouth drawn into a thoughtful frown. "Maybe. Or maybe I *don't* have attention deficit disorder."

He smirked. "Can I ask you a question?"

"You can ask." She buttered a slice of warm pumpernickel raisin bread and bit into it. The heavenly flavor danced over her taste buds, a precursor to the soon-to-be-devoured chocolate dessert. "Doesn't mean I'll answer."

"Fair enough."

"So?"

"What's with you and the succub—" He flushed, as if realizing what he almost said. "Er, I mean, what's with you and your mother?"

She started to answer, but he cut her off with a raised hand. "I've heard some stuff from Gramps, but, well, I always put his comments down to bitterness from their divorce. And now you've made it plain that there's no love lost between you two either."

"Back up the assumption truck, pal." She dropped the bread onto her plate and rubbed her fingers through her napkin. "I admit I hate her sense of values. I hate the way she conducts her life, and I hate her compulsions about marriage. But she's still my mother, and I love her. That's my cross to bear. My life would be a lot easier if I did hate her."

She stared out the window at a family of white swans gliding across the shimmering Long Island Sound. On a deep sigh, she added, "Love gets me into more trouble than hate ever could."

Dante's glass clinked against his bread plate, drawing her attention in time to watch him drain the contents in one huge gulp. Swallowing, he offered her a slow nod, his brow pleated. "I know exactly what you mean."

Chapter Three

"Tell me about your relationship with my grandfather," Dante ordered as he sliced into his perfectly grilled rib eye.

At least something about today was easy to swallow. He still couldn't believe Gramps had forced this partnership on him. Hanging around Nicole Fleming would definitely keep him on his toes over the next nine months. Now might be a good time to nudge her off balance and gain an edge on their slippery slope.

She didn't answer right away. Maybe the onion slices in her salad were to blame, but he could have sworn she sniffed back tears. "He married my mother when I was six." Her voice was a croaky whisper, but grew stronger when she added, "He was my favorite of all my mom's husbands. Aside from my father."

"He was only married to your mother for three years."

She offered him a tremulous smile. "Thirty-eight months.

22

The best thirty-eight months of my life. Papa Joe took me to my first Yankees game."

He snorted. "Oh, well, then I can understand your enthusiasm."

With a look of disgust, she clucked her tongue. "It was more than that. He took an *interest* in me. We did so many things together. He added a sidecar to his Harley, and every Sunday we'd hop on that bike, bound for adventure. We'd head out east, meet up with some of his friends, and spend the day at the beach or a park, or fishing on the piers."

The steak he swallowed left a bitter aftertaste. He'd loved sharing all those activities with Gitan. Long ago and far away. Before he'd learned the truth.

He cast an angry glance upward. *Come on, old man. I don't have time to waste on some silly treasure hunt. Why couldn't you just leave me a quick bit of cash without my having to leap through hoops of fire to gain it?*

"For someone like me," Nicole said, jerking Dante back into the conversation. "Papa Joe was a godsend."

"Someone like you?"

She picked up a roll and proceeded to rip it into pieces. "My mom's not exactly the warm-and-fuzzy type. Oh, she'll melt over a basket of orphaned kittens, but when it comes to people . . ." She shrugged. "People are stepping stones for my mother. She's a habitual bride. As of last June, she was on husband number seven."

"Unlucky in love, eh?"

"Yeah, but lucky in settlements." The pieces of roll became shards, and her fingers dug through the wreckage. "While I was growing up, she always insisted, once the divorce was final, that her exes weren't ever to contact me again. She claimed it was less traumatic for me that way. I would've disagreed, but what would I know about my feelings?"

What indeed? Another glance at the ceiling brought an intriguing thought. What if the old man had insisted on Dante joining forces with Nicole so she might provide insight into how best to handle Gitan? After all, who knew more about loving someone else's child than Gramps?

Yes, talking to Nicole might definitely provide a new face to his dilemma. The face of a confused teenager, a boy who couldn't understand why his life had changed so drastically.

Sweeping her hand over the tablecloth, Nicole gathered the dough onto her bread plate. "Papa Joe was the only one to disobey Mom's edict."

"You kept in touch with him all these years?"

She nodded. "On my tenth birthday I got a card in the mail. No return address, no signature, but I knew it was from him."

"How?"

She pierced a lettuce leaf with her fork, but never moved the food toward her mouth. "Instead of a signature, the card had that dodo he used to doodle. Do you remember? Anytime you caught Papa Joe with a pencil in his hand, he'd draw that silly stick-legged bird. The pointy beak, feathers that looked more like wisps of hair, and google eyes, all atop a chicken's body."

"I remember."

Funny, he hadn't thought about that dodo for years. Yet how could anyone forget? That stupid bird was Gramps' personal stamp, gracing every written correspondence, from birthday cards to legal documents. Dante wouldn't be surprised to learn the old man had drawn it next to the notary seal on his will.

"The following year I received another card with the same drawing. But when I turned twelve, he drew a balloon popping out of the dodo's beak with a phone number and the words 'Call Collect.'" She made quote marks in the air, with curled fingers on the left, and the lettuce leaf still dangling from her fork on the right. "So the next time Mom was on one of her weekend dates, I called."

"And?"

At last she slid the fork between her lips, chewed, and then swallowed. "We talked for about two hours in that first phone call. After that, whenever Mom went away, I called Papa Joe. I told him all the things my mother didn't care about. My game-winning triple, my first kiss, the day I got my driver's license. Papa Joe heard about every milestone in my life."

With a solemn head shake, he clucked his tongue. "I can't believe it."

"What? That I kept in touch with your grandfather?"

"No. That you could have scored a game-winning triple."

She laughed. Nicole Fleming laughed *completely*. Her entire body shook. She didn't attempt to stifle the volume for the benefit of other patrons. When she slapped the table with glee, the dishes and silverware tinkled at the force. Half a dozen heads swerved in their direction, eyes wide with curiosity. Too caught up in her own amusement, Nicole never noticed.

Gramps used to laugh like that.

The memory struck like lightning, illuminating his brain in one quick flash. Was it an affect? She'd have to be a heckuva good actress. Then again, if she had any of her mother's genes in her, that wasn't too much of a stretch.

Why did he keep forgetting the two women were linked by blood? Better to stick to the business at hand, learn what he could about her relationship with Gramps, retrieve the treasure, and get away from her as fast as possible.

He waited for her laughter to subside, and then pulled his envelope from his pocket. "Shall we compare notes?"

"I thought you'd never ask." She picked up her matching envelope. "Who goes first?"

"Ladies," he said with a wave of his hand. "Always."

"Okay!" With one swipe she rendered the envelope as useless as the unfortunate bread from earlier. After yanking out the pages, she ran a hesitant finger over the scripted words, as if absorbing some secret message.

"Well?" he prompted.

"Okay, okay." On a sigh, she began, " '*Dear Clipper*—' "

" 'Clipper'?" Laughter erupted before he could stifle it. "Who or what is a 'Clipper'?"

She lifted her gaze from the letter, one eyebrow arched. "Didn't Papa Joe give you a nickname?"

"Sure, but it wasn't anything as lame as 'Clipper.' "

She leaned forward on folded arms. "Yeah? So, what was it? Grumpy? How about Cranky? Or Snotty?"

"Would you get on with this?" Was she always so scatterbrained? No wonder Gramps had given them nine months to find the treasure. They'd probably need every second just to keep Nicole focused on the task at hand.

"No, wait, I know. Was your nickname . . ." Her grin turned malevolent, in an exaggerated, goofy way. "Fluffy?"

In reply, he balled his napkin and tossed it at her nose. She flinched as the missile bounced off her face harmlessly and landed with a soft plop in front of her.

"Oh, yeah. You definitely throw like a Fluffy."

"Just for that I'm not going to tell you my nickname."

"Fine." She gave an exaggerated shrug. "Then I'll just call you Fluffy."

His spine went rigid at the thought. "Okay, fine. Iron-man."

She tilted her head, looking at him from a new angle. "Excuse me?"

"Ironman." At her continued blank look, he added, "You know. Like that old Black Sabbath song."

Her eyes rolled so high, they momentarily disappeared beneath her lids. "Oh, but *Clipper* is lame."

"Of course it's lame. It sounds like the newest Muppet on *Sesame Street.*"

"It's not from *Sesame Street,*" she snapped. "Papa Joe named me after Joe DiMaggio."

He took his time, drinking in every detail of her face. God, she was so pretty. Too pretty. Finally, when she squirmed under his scrutiny, he noted, "Strange. I don't see the slightest resemblance."

"You haven't seen me on the baseball diamond." With a wide arc, she mimed swinging a bat and clipped the busboy who approached.

"Sorry," she murmured and sat back, toying with the napkin on her lap.

Mumbling his own apology, the young man reached to clear away the dirty lunch dishes. While he worked, she said nothing and Dante found himself staring out the window at the seagulls swooping over the pier in search of an afternoon snack.

The moment the server stepped away with his cluttered tray, she leaned forward again, hands clasped on the white table-cloth. "And were you Ironman because you resembled Ozzy Osbourne? Or because you hold yourself so stiffly?"

Did he? Instinctively, he straightened, and then, realizing what he was doing, forced himself to relax into a slouch. "The name comes from the first time I met Gramps. I was thirteen. He'd divorced his wife in New York, your mother I guess, and flown down to my parents' house in Key West."

"Is that where you grew up?"

"Who says I've grown up?"

She pointed her teaspoon at him. "Excellent point."

"But yes, to answer your question. I lived in Key West until about eight years ago." Leaving the old life, the *old wife,* be-hind for a fresh start. At Gramps' insistence. Now he wondered if Nicole living here had anything to do with Gramps' advice. Made sense—in a twisted Gramps sort of way.

"I've never been to Key West," she said, resting an elbow on the table, her chin atop her fist. "But I've heard it's the clos-est place to paradise this side of the Atlantic."

"As an adult, I'd agree with that assessment. But as a kid, it wasn't that fabulous. My mom worried about skin cancer long before the medical world made the term the buzzword it is today. So spending hours lazing in the sun was out of the question. Take the beach out of the equation and there's not much to do. Plus, in those days, my dad was a new citizen, trying to find his niche in his adopted country, which made money tight. I was the only kid in the neighborhood without a bike. So I scouted junkyards for parts and built my own."

"And that's why your grandfather named you Ironman?"

The memory flooded back as if replayed at the table directly across from him. "Gramps stepped out of a taxi one Saturday morning, strolled up the driveway, and found me attempting to attach a seven-speed hub to my bike. Even though he was all dressed up in this *Saturday Night Fever* white suit, he knelt down next to me and dug in to the project. By the time we got the hub on, he was coated with grease and grass stains. The old man didn't care."

Her full lips curved into a lush smile. "My mother used to go nuts over his laundry. She'd spend a fortune on a new shirt and he'd wear it while mowing the lawn or painting my bedroom."

"Your mom may not have appreciated it, but his helping me went a long way to earning *my* respect. And he seemed pretty impressed with me too. When I told Gramps how I'd built the whole bike from scratch, he said, 'You're a regular Ironman, ain't ya, kid?' That's how I got my nickname. Years later, I even named my business Ironman."

"What type of business do you own?"

"Ironman Motor Works. I customize motorcycles and sports cars."

Her head cocked to one side, and a blond curl bounced against her cheek. "Like those guys on television? I once saw them turn a car into a dragon for some movie premiere or something. Can you do stuff like that?"

He shrugged. "Probably. Why? You want me to design a car for you?"

"Sure," she scoffed. "Take my beat-up Civic and paint pin-stripes on it. Then it'll be easy to pick out in the junkyard."

She looked down at the letter, and then up into his face, and then back to the letter.

"What?" he asked. "Did you come up with something?"

She frowned, scratched her head, twirled the gold stud earring in her right lobe. "Yes and no. It's more a feeling, a suspicion, than a clue. Have you ever heard of the Iron Horse?"

He thought for a moment. "No, can't say I have."

"That was Lou Gehrig's nickname. He played for the Yankees in the thirties."

"So?"

"So, I'm named for a Yankee hero of the forties and your nickname is awfully close to the nickname of a Yankee from a few years earlier. It could just be coincidence—"

"No. Gramps didn't believe in coincidences and would never have set up a coincidence for us to follow."

She jerked her head toward the sealed letter near his place setting. "Open yours. Let's see how he addressed you."

Reluctantly, he picked up the envelope, slit it open with his butter knife, and flipped out the folded pages. He didn't get past the first two lines:

Hey Ironman.
Ask Nicole to tell you about Lou Gehrig . . .

He slapped the letter onto the table and stared at Nicole with new suspicion. "How did you know about Lou Gehrig?"

She shrugged. "Everyone who knows baseball history knows Lou Gehrig. Didn't you ever see *Pride of the Yankees* with Gary Cooper? 'Today . . . day . . . day . . . day, I consider myself . . . self . . . self . . . self . . . the luckiest man on the face of the earth . . .' Classic movie."

Time to reel her in again. He pounded his index finger on the chicken scratch his grandfather had scrawled. "But what does this Lou Gehrig reference mean?"

"Well, the obvious links would be between Joe DiMaggio, since that's my nickname, and Gehrig, who shares at least part of your nickname."

"And those are?"

Her brow wrinkled in thought, she heaved a sigh. "I don't know. They both played for the Yankees."

"Terrific," he muttered. "For all we know the treasure is buried under home plate at Yankee Stadium."

She spun the gold ball in her earlobe, round and round, round and round. "Which means we'll have to keep digging."

"Okay. So what else does your letter say? After the 'Dear Clipper' part?"

Chapter Four

Nicole picked up the page, shook it as if preparing to present a speech, and read aloud:

" *'Dear Clipper . . .'* " She waited a beat for another acerbic comment from Dante, but when he remained silent, she plowed on.

" *'I wish I could say that rumors about my demise are exaggerated, but apparently, that's not the case. Get your tears over with quick because I have a lot I want to tell you and I don't want you bawling through my heartfelt words.*

'My daughter, Maura, was the child of my youth. She was born when I was barely twenty years old. Don't get me wrong, I love her like mad. But I made mistakes with her. I know I did. She knows I did. Despite those mistakes, she gave me a terrific grandson in Dante. So somewhere along the road, I must've done something right.' "

32

"Get outta here," Dante interjected in an ursine growl. "Gramps didn't really write that, did he?"

Was that so hard for him to believe? "Umm . . . yeah, he did." Frowning, she held out the page to him. "See?"

After he had a chance to read the passage himself, she faced the page around to her eyes again, and continued.

" 'Then I met your mother. I'd consider that the blackest day of my life except for one thing. If I hadn't met her, I'd never have known you.' "

Her tongue grew thick with emotion, and she stumbled over the next few words.

" 'You, Nicole, became the daughter of my old age, the daughter a man could be proud of. I like to think I'm one of the reasons you're so different from Rhoda. Maybe my influence made you more aware of what's important in life.

'I'm just glad she never knew that you were the best thing about our marriage. If she'd known how much you meant to me, she might have destroyed you out of spite. I ain't being melodramatic when I say that, either.

'Remember what she did to my autographed picture of Tina Louise? Even hanging it in the boathouse wasn't good enough for her. Poor Ginger from* Gilligan's Island, *smeared with motor oil, paint thinner eating her fabulous face. A tragedy. That was the beginning of the end for us, I think. I can't respect a woman who'll desecrate rare beauty out of envy.' "

Dante snorted. "The man had style. I'll grant you that."

She frowned at his interruption—again. "Do you want to hear this or not?"

Like Henry VIII ordering her execution, he waved a hand. "Go on."

" 'I know it sounds like I'm sending you and Dante on a scavenger hunt. In a way, I am. Problem is, Nicole, you've turned into a fraidy cat.' "

This time, Dante's snort came out more like a strangled chuckle, but she ignored it.

" 'You go to work, come home, maybe spend some time with that friend of yours—Farrah, wasn't it?—who, by the way, has a husband now. Nice as Jason is, I'm sure there are times he gets tired of having a sidekick to contend with. There's a reason they say three's a crowd. The minute it became Charles, Diana, and Camilla, pffft! That marriage was doomed. You can bet your boots the Seven Dwarfs didn't move in with Snow White and Prince Charming for the same reason.

'In any event, your life's in a rut. And Nicole, honey, I think that kind of life sucks. 'Cuz it's a waiting game. Waiting for something to happen, waiting for your life to begin. Pretty soon you'll discover you've waited too long. And I can't bear the thought of you looking back on your life one day, wondering where all your time went.

'While I don't agree with your mother's sort of finagling, I gotta admit, it's one way to get you out of that house so you can spread your wings and fly.

'As for Dante, he has other issues I need him to address before he can move on with his life. What better way to kill two birds with one stone, eh?

'You probably hate me for doing this to you, but I love you,

Nicole Elizabeth Fleming. And I need to know you'll be all right when I'm gone. This treasure hunt is the best way I know.

'*Think of this like a jigsaw puzzle. Between you and Dante, you have all the pieces you need to solve it.*

'*Take care of yourself. Place your faith in my grandson and make sure he puts his faith in you. You'll only find the treasure if you learn to work together.*

Love,

Papa Joe.' "

She placed the letter on the table and gave Dante her full attention. "Thoughts? Ideas? Suspicions? I'll take anything you've got right now."

Except analysis on Papa Joe's "fraidy cat" commentary.

He clasped his hands on the table. "For starters, I'd like to know what your mother is holding over your head."

Okay, I really don't want to discuss that, either . . .

She steeled her spine and pursed her lips in distaste. "My mother's issues with me are none of your business."

His brow pleated. "Do I look stupid to you? Whatever she's threatening you with is written all over that letter." He pounded a finger on the pages. "It's why Gramps is sending you on this treasure hunt. I think I have a right to know what it is."

She folded her arms over her chest and glared. "Fine. You tell me your secret, and I'll tell you mine."

"I'll tell you mine *when and if* you need to know about it. So far, Gramps hasn't mentioned much about my problem in your letter."

"No, just that you had 'issues' you needed to address. So? What are they?"

"Let's concentrate on you for now." The bite in his tone could cut lead.

"Chicken."

He grinned, showing a perfect smile. "Nice try, but no dice. You think you can dare me into revealing something? You don't know me very well."

Despite his anger, Nicole wondered why the guy didn't smile more often. If he did, he'd have weak-kneed women stumbling all over town.

"So?" he prompted.

She had to buy time. No way was she ready to share the fact that she'd been an idiot who'd fallen blindly into her mother's trap. "I'll tell you what. Why don't we read your letter and see if that helps shed more light on our next step?"

"Chicken."

She didn't attempt to deny it. Instead, she leaned forward and slowly enunciated, "Buck, buck, buck."

Thank God her ploy worked. Laughing, he picked up his letter, shook it the way she had shaken hers, and began to read:

" '*Hey Ironman.*

'*Ask Nicole to tell you about Lou Gehrig. Go on. I'll wait. What the hell else am I gonna do? I'm dead. At least I should be dead. Or you shouldn't be reading this. But since I've tried to convince Nicole you're an honorable guy and I've paid that lawyer a boatload of money to follow my instructions to the letter, I'm going to assume I'm really dead. So, go on. Ask her.*

'Done yet? Okay, good. Here's the deal. There were never two finer ballplayers in the history of the game than Lou Gehrig and Joe DiMaggio, not just for their skills on the diamond. Each of them had his own strengths, his own weaknesses. But when they played together on the same team, they worked together to become a winning force.

'You know why I nicknamed you Ironman? It's because you can manipulate steel into all kinds of useful items. From that bike you'd built as a kid to the stuff you do now. But there's another side of you I've been seeing lately, a side I don't like.

'Ever since you and Linda split, you've taken the Ironman nickname to new levels. You've encased your heart in that steel you manipulate. You've forgotten what's important in life.

'You used to be the guy who could make a roomful of people laugh with one joke, one comment, one look. You used to smile. Remember how to do that, Dante? Or have your facial muscles atrophied into a permanent scowl?' "

Now, Nicole had to stifle a giggle, and Dante glared at her with the same sharpness she'd used on him only minutes ago. "I'm sorry, but you have to admit. Your grandfather always cut right to the chase."

"Should I continue?"

"Oh, please do."

" 'It's time to spread your wings, Dante. So Linda wasn't the paragon of virtue you thought. Big deal. You ain't the first guy to be taken in by a pair of pretty eyes and you won't be the last. Your caged door is open, son. Spread your wings and soar with the seagulls.

'Remember that life is precious and every moment we're

given should be lived to the fullest. Take it from someone who's apparently just died: Life is too short to be cranky.

'Find your joy again. Nicole can help you with that. She's one of the most joyful people I know. And living with the succubus all these years, she'd have reason to be miserable. Trust her with your burden. Show her she can trust you to share hers. If you two learn to put aside your animosity and work together, you can achieve a great deal. At least, that's my hope.

Love,

Gramps'"

Dante placed the sheets of stationery facedown.

"That's it?" Nicole asked.

Hands flipped in surrender over the pages. "Th-th-th-th-th-that's all, folks."

She itched to move his hands, to verify he hadn't held anything back. But she fiddled with the salt and pepper shakers instead. "No other mention of Lou Gehrig or Joe DiMaggio?"

"Nope. Just the opening bit."

"But that doesn't make sense," she sputtered. "We still don't know what it's supposed to mean."

His eyes widened beneath sooty lashes. Why did God give men perfect lashes that never needed mascara? Was He in cahoots with Max Factor?

"No one said Gramps was going to make this easy on us," Dante said. "In fact, reading between the lines, I'd say he made this treasure hunt especially difficult so we'd have no choice but to learn to rely on each other."

Irritation heated her itch to a slow burn. "So what else do you see 'between the lines'?"

He started to reply, but the waiter reappeared and set the chocolate bag between them on the table.

All thoughts of baseball and treasure and Papa Joe flitted from her mind at the sight of the delicate dark chocolate shell shaped like a paper bag, stuffed with velvety chocolate mousse and sweet berries and topped with whipped cream. Decadence, pure and simple.

"Hold that thought," she told Dante. "This dessert is too good to be glossed over. What do you say we table this discussion until later?"

With her chocolate craving satisfied at last, Nicole sipped cinnamon-scented decaf and ran through her entire mental catalog of New York Yankees history.

"I guess the main similarity between DiMaggio and Gehrig was their gentlemanly behavior," she told Dante. "Lou Gehrig was superhumble. I mean, think about it. This was a guy who spent most of his career under the shadow of Babe Ruth. No matter what the record—base hits, RBIs, even homers—Babe was first, Lou would be second or third. The year Lou was awarded MVP by the Yanks? That was the same year Babe had his sixty-home-runs-in-one-season record. Talk about a buzzkill. But Lou never complained and never tried to puff himself up. And in the end, what accolades did he get? The disease that killed him is now named after him. Yippee."

"And DiMaggio?"

She considered Joltin' Joe for a moment. "Another guy who lived in Babe Ruth's shadow, but for a different reason. DiMaggio had the laws of physics working against him. The way Yankee Stadium is built favors left-handed batters like the Babe. It's nearly impossible for a rightie like Joe to hit a ball into deep center or left and send it screaming over the fence."

"Oh? Why is that?"

"I'm not exactly sure. Something about a forty-five-degree angle versus a ninety-degree angle on the foul lines." She offered him an apologetic smile. "Physics was never my strong suit. Still, DiMaggio's the only baseball player ever to be selected for the All-Star game every year he played professionally. And of course, you know about him and Marilyn Monroe, right?"

"They were married, weren't they?"

"For about a year. He never stopped loving her. After her death, he established a standing order with a local florist. Half a dozen red roses placed on her grave three times a week, every week, until he died. After he retired from baseball, he did commercials, a couple of movies, and opened the Joe DiMaggio Children's Hospital in Miami."

"So we've got one guy who had a disease named after him, the other a hospital."

She shook her head slowly. "But I honestly don't see how any of that information points to a treasure for us."

Dante pushed his cup to the corner and expelled air through pursed lips. "Let's move on from baseball for now. Maybe we should get back to your mother. What's this deal Gramps was talking about?"

"I've already told you." She folded her arms over her chest. "I'm not going to discuss that with you."

"Come on, how bad can it be?" Dante asked for what must have been the thousandth time.

Once again, Nicole shook her head like a stubborn mule. "No. I don't want to talk about my mother."

Minutes ticked by in silence. Soon they'd lose hours, and then days, and then weeks. Time would escape them too quickly if he didn't rein in Nicole. With a deep breath to calm the impatience twitching him, he clasped a hand in hers.

"Look. This is ridiculous. We have to stop wasting time. Knowing Gramps, you and I are going to need to know every minuscule detail of each other's lives up to this point. If you so much as scraped your knee at Lou Gehrig Elementary School, you've gotta tell me. For all we know, the treasure is buried under the jungle gym there."

"You're right." She sighed. "What exactly did Papa Joe tell you about my mother?"

Thank God. She was willing to talk. He'd have to take this conversation slow and easy. Didn't want to spook her.

"Almost nothing. I was a kid when he split from your mother. What little info I learned, Gramps told me when I was going through my own divorce."

He stopped, considering how much he should tell her at this stage. Well, maybe if he opened up a little toward her, she'd feel a need to reciprocate. "I guess my marital experiences left me a little bitter."

Nicole snorted. "Gee. You think?"

"I won't apologize," he retorted. "If you'd been through—" This time he censored himself. There was a difference between sharing a little history and baring his soul. No way would he cross that line with her. Not now, not ever.

"In any case," he said instead, "Gramps told me a little about you and how your mother used to manipulate his feelings for you to get what she wanted out of him."

"Yeah, my mother's a real piece of work." She sighed again, this time with all the defeat of the losing Super Bowl team. "I live in the house I grew up in. My parents bought the place when they first married. Papa Joe lived there too, after my dad left. My house is the one place in the whole world that holds special memories for me. It's my birthright, all I want from my mother and her many-marriages fortune. I made the mistake of telling her so."

Ah. The plot grew clearer. "So, naturally, because you want it so badly, she's not ready to turn it over to you."

She nodded. "We made a deal. Correction . . . my mother made the deal. I agreed in a moment of weakness. I was young and stupid and naive and sentimental, all qualities my mother loves to manipulate."

"Even with her only daughter?"

She gave a mirthless chuckle. "My mother's colder than a polar bear's feet. Ten years ago, she wanted to sell the house. She wanted me to move to Boca Raton with her." Her voice cracked, and she sniffed. "I couldn't. My life was here. All my friends were here. Everything I know and love is here."

"So what kind of deal did she offer you?"

"She agreed to allow me to live here until I turn thirty. Af-ter I hit that magic number, I can buy the house at fair market value or I'm out on the street. My thirtieth birthday is a mere seven months away."

Cute. And very sharp. After all, what did a twenty-year-old kid know about fair market value?

"How much is the place worth?"

"As is," she said flatly, "with the bulkhead and the docking rights, three point two million dollars."

Awe had him whistling through his teeth. "No wonder you need a treasure."

She shrugged. "I never realized what she was up to when I made the deal. I mean, my house is little more than an old bungalow. But it sits on three acres of prime beachfront real estate. I always thought I was purchasing an outdated shack. So I purposely didn't make any improvements to the property. For the last ten years, I've lived with this Brady Bunch era decor, without any kind of permanent update to the house because I thought I could outwit my mother. I should have known better. Two weeks ago, she served me with an eviction notice."

To cover a surprised gulp, he coughed. "You're kidding."

"No, I'm not. I've got six months or so to raise the full amount or I'm out on my too-curvy butt."

Leering, he waggled his brows. "There's no such thing as too curvy." Whatever response he expected from the weak joke, he didn't get.

Instead, she slapped a palm against her temple repeatedly while murmuring, "Stupid, stupid, stupid . . ."

Did she mean him? Or herself? "I don't suppose you can parcel out the property?"

"Nope. Everything's still in my mother's name. She can do what she wants with the property, no matter what I'd like. She caught me good."

What else could he say? "I'm sorry, Nicole. Really."

"Yeah, well, so am I." She placed her chin in her palm. "My mother is the meanest, most vindictive woman in the world."

"And arrogant, if what Gramps told me is true," he added sympathetically. "Though, I admit, I never heard about the Tina Louise picture until now. Not that that anecdote does anything more than clinch my suspicions about your mother's vanity."

Nicole leaned back, staring at the ceiling fan spinning slowly above them. "God, how she hated that picture. I remember when he first showed it to her. His friend, Rusty, had given it to him for his birthday—" She stopped short. "Oh. My. God."

She fumbled for the two letters, lifted one. Then she returned to the other. She laid them side by side, as if comparing them. Finally she looked up. "Do you notice anything unusual about the metaphors he uses in our letters?"

"Yeah, the common thread about spreading our wings and learning to fly. But what does it mean?"

She didn't answer at first. Simply sat there, twirling the earring, reading the two letters, her face a mask of intense concentration. "No." The words came out in a mere whisper. "He couldn't have meant that. Could he?"

"What?" Dante prompted, leaning forward to stare at the papers, to discern what she might have seen. "What's wrong?"

"Oh, you devil, you," she muttered to the pages.

"What?" Dante repeated. "Did you figure it out?"

"I figured out where we have to go next," she replied, and then smirked. "How's your heart?"

"It's fine. Why?"

"I think your grandfather is about to send your heart into overdrive."

"What do you mean? How?"

Laughing, she gestured to the letter. "That bit about Tina Louise? See how it's followed by the advice that I should dive into adventure and learn to fly? He's referring to Rusty."

"Rusty who? How do you know that?"

"Rusty Bridges. He owns a company called Drop Zone Long Island. Apparently, in order to learn more about the treasure, you and I will have to jump out of an airplane at thirteen thousand feet."

Chapter Five

"He knew you'd figure it out." A beaming Arthur "Rusty" Bridges pulled Nicole into a bony embrace that both welcomed and disturbed her.

When had Rusty grown so old? His fiery red hair had dulled to silver, and the man himself had dwarfed to five foot four, tops. Butterflies flitted around Nicole's stomach. As a child, she'd always viewed Rusty as loud and large. Now, using an adult's perspective, his voice was a grating whisper, the top of his head barely reached her chin, and his frame had less meat than a soup chicken.

Uncomfortable with what the years had done, she gazed around the office of Drop Zone Long Island and found contentment in the familiar. Dust motes still danced through chinks of sunlight filtering in the greasy plate-glass windows. That same sunlight glinted off dirty mason jars filled with corroded bolts and screws. Despite the passage of decades, Rusty's waiting room had remained the cluttered, cobwebbed catch-all she remembered with nostalgia.

How many afternoons had she spent on the old vinyl car seat that served as a couch? She bet she'd still find the evidence of her many drippy fudge bars on its faded blue surface.

Every time they arrived there, Papa Joe would hand her a frozen fudge bar to keep her happy while he spent time in Rusty's hangar. Unlike now, in those days the office had no air-conditioning. The heat of the summer sun would burn through the tarred roof, causing Nicole to wilt and the chocolaty ice to melt in dime-sized droplets all over her clothes and the seat.

"He told me when he set this up," Rusty continued, wiping a greasy rag across his prune-wrinkled face. " 'Clipper's gonna stroll in here one day with this handsome buck beside her. They're gonna ask to skydive. That's when you'll know I'm dead. No tears now, Rusty. Just do as I tell you. When they show up, make 'em do the full accelerated freefall program before you give them any information.' "

"The full accelerated freefall program?" Nicole's heart shot up into her throat and she took a step back, slamming smack-dab into Dante's hard chest.

His arm wrapped around her shoulders to steady her, lending balance against her pitching emotions.

When composure returned, she stepped forward again. "We can't just do one tandem skydive?"

Rusty shook his head. "Nope. The full accelerated. You had breakfast, didn't ya?"

"Like I'd incur your wrath by showing up here if I hadn't," she retorted.

She remembered every word of the diatribe assigned to potential customers who attempted to jump on an empty stomach. Or worse, with alcohol on their breath.

"Good girl." He tossed an issue of *Popular Mechanics* onto a pile of magazines perched precariously atop a three-legged table. "You'll be here about six hours. So, let's not waste time. We'll start you on ground training and jumping with instructors. You'll learn stable body position, altitude awareness, how to activate your parachute, and how to perform a radio-assisted landing. By the time we're finished with you, you'll both be able to perform dive exits out of the plane, backloops, one-eighties and three-sixties. Sound excitin'?"

"Can't wait," Dante replied through a clenched-teeth smile.

Chortling, Rusty slapped his back. "Come on, Dante. Your grandfather could do all that and more. You're not about to let the old man down, are ya?"

"Just show us where to go," Dante growled.

Rusty grinned, his protruding eyes reminding Nicole of carved gargoyles she'd once seen guarding the eaves of a Gold Coast mansion. "Right this way, kids."

Five and a half hours later, Nicole and Dante prepared for their final jump of the day. Dressed in orange jumpsuits, they stood inside the Cessna 207, packs strapped to their backs, goggles covering their eyes, and soft helmets on their heads.

"This is it, kids," Rusty shouted over the roar of the plane's engine. "If you two nail your solo, you'll have accomplished the tasks Joe set up for today. After the jump, come back to the office at Home Base, and I'll fill you in on the message he left for yas. You ready?"

Too terrified to speak, Nicole nodded and took Dante's hand. He squeezed her fingers, and she clung to his strength. Despite the hours of training and the dozens of jumps they'd already taken in tandem with instructors, Nicole still shivered in apprehension of this last leap. Papa Joe's directives insisted that she and Dante take this final jump together, holding hands as they "soared in the wild blue yonder."

She gulped when Rusty slid the jump door open and nearly lost her breakfast when Dante stepped to the opening in the plane without hesitation. Swallowing her fear, she forced her feet to move forward until she stood beside him. Wind whipped the fabric around her legs with a loud *whap-whap-whap* that matched the rhythm of her frantic heartbeat.

"Off you go, kids," Rusty shouted. "See you thirteen thousand feet from now."

His hand landed on her shoulder, and then her feet left solid ground. Cold air slapped her cheeks, freezing her terrified expression. Her heart soared into her throat and blocked the scream-seeking release.

Dante became her lifeline, her only link to Earth. She gripped his hand hard enough to break his fingers. If she could've flown close enough to cling to his chest and press her face into his neck like some helpless cartoon heroine, she would have. Instead, she closed her eyes while they hurtled toward the ground at blinding speed.

Her mind instinctively counted out the time as they'd been instructed and, after the longest forty seconds of her life, she broke away from Dante and pulled her cord. Never in all her days had she felt the flood of relief that washed over her at the *whoosh* of the opening parachute.

A second later her bones jerked and she slowed down enough to open her eyes. She lost track of Dante while she wafted downward, helpless as an autumn leaf on a November breeze.

Soon only sky surrounded her. Silence reigned. The roar of the plane's engine disappeared as if swallowed by a cloud. Even her heartbeat stopped pounding in her ears. Peace enveloped her, and she could well imagine Papa Joe smiling down upon her, proud as a new daddy.

What's next, old man? Bronc busting? Volcano jumping? Scuba diving with sharks?

Trees drew nearer, and then the ground came firmly into view. She studied the horizon, concentrating on her upcoming landing.

Her bottom hit the ground squarely, and she rolled away from the falling sheets of silk. The chute fluttered down beside her, a ghostly tablecloth covering dandelion-scattered grass. She lay there, catching her breath, regaining equilibrium, then slowly sat up and removed the helmet and goggles.

A few yards to her right, Dante unhooked his pack, tossed his helmet and goggles to the ground, and walked toward her. Safe at last, she rose, unhooked her own pack, and ran straight into his open arms.

He wrapped her in a hug of iron, kissing the top of her head. "How do you feel?"

"Like a bazillion dollars," she exclaimed. "You?"

"Grateful that I'm walking out of this alive." He pulled away and took her hand. "Come on. Let's head to Home Base and find out what Gramps has in store for us next."

They trudged back to the hangar and found Rusty stepping out of the aircraft with the pilot beside him. Spotting them approaching, he clapped. "Well done, kids. Well done. Joe would be mighty proud of you two."

Overcome with emotion, Nicole rushed forward and kissed his scruffy cheeks. "Thanks, Rusty. Today was awesome!"

"You liked it, eh?" He turned to Dante. "What about you? You sorry you came along for this?"

Shaking his head, Dante grinned. "She's right. I've never experienced anything like it."

"Well, that's good to hear," Rusty replied. "I suppose you're wondering what the old man wants from you next, eh?"

Nicole shared an amused smile with Dante. "The thought crossed our minds."

"Okay, here's what Joe wanted me to tell yas: 'To keep and nurture a treasure such as mine, a man needs to know how to soar with the eagles, how to keep his head above water, how to see the greater plan of the world, how to value what is most important in life. You've just learned how to soar with the eagles. Go to Ditch Plains Beach as soon as possible and find a man named Moondog Monroe. He'll teach you how to keep your head above water.'"

"Moondog Monroe?" Dante turned toward Nicole, brow puckered in confusion. "Do you know him?"

She nodded, her thoughts with Papa Joe and the devious wheels inside his head. "I remember Moondog. Twenty years ago, he was known as the oldest active surfer on Montauk Point."

Rich, full laughter haunted Dante's dreams. Through the shroud of sleep he saw Nicole's face, animated, blue eyes wide with wonder behind overlarge goggles, as they plummeted hand-in-hand thirteen thousand feet to Earth.

Brrrring! The phone rang near Dante's ear.

Lost in the sparkle of her laughter, he fumbled for the noise-box and the receiver. What time was it? He shot a bleary glance at the green LCD display of his clock radio: 1:45 A.M. Who'd be calling him at this hour?

Somebody was about to hear some colorful language for waking him. His first attempt brought the mouthpiece to his ear, and he juggled the receiver to speak into the right end.

"Who is this?" he barked out.

A brief pause. Then the very hesitant, "Hey."

Dante's heart shot up his throat, and he struggled to clear the fog from his head. "Gitan, is that you?"

"Yeah."

He willed his heart to return to its chamber, breathing slowly and deeply. "Where are you? And does your mom know you called me?"

"No. But ask me if I care. She's out with that guy, Curt, and probably won't come home 'til tomorrow."

Not again. He sat up in bed, reached for the lamp. A quick turn of the screw illuminated the room, temporarily blinding him. He blinked several times, focusing his vision, but leaving his mind in a hurricane of emotions.

Dammit, Linda, he's your son. Not a dog you can leave alone whenever you and Curt are looking for a little action. Bad enough you left me to do the dirty work about your nasty little secret . . .

He stopped the thought before a foul mood completely overtook him and repeated the mantra he'd developed over the years. *Not now. I will not take the sins of the mother out on the boy. Not now. Not ever.*

There in the solitude of his bedroom, he practiced smiling until he could fake a happy tone. "What's up? How are things going down there?"

"This town sucks," Gitan exclaimed in the same hoarse whisper. "I hate it here. And I hate Curt. He's always bossing me around, like he's my father or something."

Because he is *your father.*

He bit back the thought, reminding himself Gitan knew nothing about the murky details of his parentage. He *would* know, after next weekend. Lucky Dante had been handed the distasteful responsibility of telling him. But he'd do it face-to-face, not over the phone.

"Listen, Gitan, we'll talk about all this stuff when you come up next week. In the meantime, hang in there. Okay?"

"Yeah, sure. Why should you care?"

Good God. Why did the kid have to sound so miserable?

Dante couldn't just hang up now. His exhausted brain

scrambled for something cheerful to say. "Hey, guess what I did yesterday?"

"What?"

"I jumped out of an airplane."

"Bull." Gitan's tone never lost its angsty edge.

"Wanna bet?" Leaving out all mention of Nicole and Gramps' will, he described the experience as best he could, summing up the day's events with, "Maybe we can do a tandem jump while you're here. You think you might like that?"

"Maybe."

Not exactly the enthusiasm he'd hoped for, but at least the crisis had passed. For now.

Ten minutes later, he hung up and climbed out of bed to throw on a pair of shorts. He padded down the circular staircase to his office and powered on his computer. Sleep would evade him for the rest of the night. Best he could do now was absorb himself in some work.

Ironman's current project, a brand spankin' new Ford Mustang Cobra, required a modified body style, hand-tooled leather interior, and a dashboard designed to resemble a deejay's turnstile setup. Some bored music celebrity wanted to outdo his business rivals with the ultimate in deejay equipment. The details of the outlandish project required breaking the laws of hydraulics as well as physics.

At this time of night, Dante welcomed the challenges. They would help take his mind off Gramps' will, Gitan's phone call, a pair of pretty blue eyes, and a laugh that uplifted his soul.

Chapter Six

At the end of Monday's workday, Nicole managed to crawl up the back steps to her kitchen door. Four hours of schlepping a couple house hunting in a car without air-conditioning had left her as wilted as month-old lettuce.

She'd begged her boss and the owner of White Pine Realty, Natasha, to let her drive her own Civic, but no. The dents and rust spots would scare customers away. Much better to sit in the soft leather seat of a shiny Lexus with an interior temperature that rivaled the Sahara than have a cool breeze blowing on you from inside a less-than-pristine Honda.

"We have an image to uphold," Natasha had whispered when handing over the keys to the company car. "Just tell them you're allergic to Freon and can't turn the AC on."

Oh, sure. They'll buy that. And then they'll plunk down twenty percent to buy a half-a-million-dollar house from me too. Not for the first time, she missed Bob Basile, the former owner of White Pine Realty. Too bad she hadn't realized what a great boss he was 'til he'd sold the place to the image czarina.

She sagged against her door, key in the lock, too drained to move. At least the day couldn't get any worse. All she wanted now was a cold drink and some mindless television to lull her into a deep sleep. With the last of her strength, she rammed her shoulder against the humidity-swollen door and stumbled inside.

"What in the name of Christian Dior are you wearing?" a faux English-accented voice demanded from her dark living room. Doom crept through the bungalow like thick, cold fog.

Correction.

The day could get a lot worse. Hurricane Rhoda had apparently made landfall in White Pine Beach.

The *click-clack* of ice-pick heels preceded the hurricane's arrival in the kitchen. "That's not the suit I bought you for Christmas, is it?" her mother offered as a greeting.

Giving up on her evening plans for peace and solitude, Nicole turned to face the perfectly coiffed, perfectly dressed, scientifically youthful woman standing a few feet away, hands on hips in her traditional "I'm very disappointed in you" stance.

Well, fine. If Mother wanted a battle from the start, Nicole was more than ready to accommodate her. "Funny. I don't recall the weatherman reporting a bad wind blowing into town."

"I take it you received the notice of eviction," her mother

said in that clenched-jaw style indicative of a few too many Botox injections.

Nicole slapped her purse onto the counter with enough force to crack the aged Formica in half. "You know darn well I got it. You made me sign for it!"

"Now, darling, it wasn't my idea. You know Louis. He insisted—"

"Cut the crap, Mother." Nicole's last nerve snapped and crackled like a live wire. "You don't do anything you don't want to do. Louis might have put the idea in your head, but you followed through on your own."

"Let's not fight, sweetie." Taking Nicole by the forearms, she pulled her into an awkward embrace.

Nicole wondered if her mother hoped to impress the cat. Everyone else had grown tired of the affection charade a long time ago.

Mother stepped back, tsking disapproval. "Hasn't anyone told you the key to success is projecting a successful image?"

First Natasha, now her mother. Why were women over fifty so preoccupied with appearance?

"Good Lord, what a mess," Mother said. "I send you a gorgeous Anne Klein suit for Christmas, and you pair it with a polyester rag from some discount store. In toxic purple, no less."

"I like toxic purple. And the blouse isn't a polyester rag. It's silk."

"If that's real silk, I'm Sophia Loren," her mother retorted, rubbing the collar between her fingers. "God, how can you wear this garbage?"

"I wear what I can afford on my salary." She yanked her collar out of her mother's perfectly manicured claws.

"Is that a Band-Aid on your sandal?"

Odd. When Dante had remarked on the makeshift shoe repair last week, she'd been happy to explain. When her mother mentioned it, the fine hairs on her nape did the cha-cha.

"Don't start," she retorted. "I like these shoes. They're comfortable and match the blouse. Not all of us keep trading up, marrying and divorcing ever-richer men, to pay for designer couture."

"That reminds me," Rhoda said, appearing unfazed by the heavy sarcasm. "Guess who's single again?"

Not again. "You have to stop, Mother. I'm not interested."

"How do you know you're not interested? You don't even know who I'm talking about. Besides, he asked about you."

"Okay, fine." She knew she'd regret it, but also knew her mother wouldn't stop the game until they'd played at least one round. "Who's single again?"

"Dr. Danny."

"Ick." The reaction flew without a moment's hesitation. At her mother's sharp look, Nicole added, "You don't find it even slightly disgusting that you're trying to fix me up with a man you dated ten years ago?"

Rhoda's perfectly manicured hand flitted in the air like a scarlet-tipped butterfly. "Pish. We only dated once. Hardly a grand affair."

"You dumped him after that one date because he hit on your waitress while you were seated at the table. What makes you think I'd want to roll those dice?"

"You're *twenty-nine*, darling." Her mother's tone left no doubt Nicole's age fell only slightly short of bald and toothless on the attraction scale. "The odds aren't in your favor anymore. After the age of thirty, you have to lower your standards if you plan to marry. Most of the men out there will be looking for replacement mothers for their children, or worse, for themselves."

"You've married enough times for both of us," Nicole replied. "Trust me. The Fleming women have filled their marital quota for the next three generations."

"No thanks to you."

"Congratulations. You're a one-woman dynamo."

She stamped her stiletto heel. "I want grandchildren while I'm still young enough to enjoy them!"

"You only want grandchildren so you can show off pictures to your mah-jongg group!" Pain shot into her brain, and she scrubbed a hand over her face, closed her eyes, and let all the bad humor out with one long exhale. "Why are you here, Mother?"

Rhoda shrugged her delicate shoulders. "Louis had a conference in New York this week. I thought we'd share some girl time. Just mother and daughter."

"Sorry, but I have to work."

"Mmm . . . too bad." Rhoda sniffed. "Are you sure you can't take a few days off? We could visit my hairdresser in the Village, do some shopping, get you some decent clothes."

She plucked the clinging skirt, damp and wrinkled, from her thighs. "What's wrong with my clothes?"

Mother said nothing. She merely stared at her own crisp,

cream-colored linen shirtdress and then at Nicole, visually comparing a pampered Persian to a battle-scarred alley cat.

Only Rhoda could get up at dawn, hop a three-hour flight, spend the day in Manhattan, and still look like a dewy-eyed model who'd stepped out of the Saks showroom.

"Darling, you dress like a ragpicker. And that hair. Look at that hair." Mother fingered the blond waves at Nicole's neck. "Didn't I tell you to see Pierre about updating your color? But once again, you ignored your mother's advice."

A light slap to Mother's fingertips and a softly hissed "Stop!" only garnered Nicole another glare of disapproval. Mother never frowned, never smiled, never puckered her brow. Mother wouldn't use any expression that might leave a line on her flawless face.

"How do you expect to attract a decent man when you look so shabby?"

"Actually, I've met a decent man. I'm seeing someone."

Oh, dear Lord, someone duct tape my mouth shut. Where did that lie come from?

"Really? How wonderful. Who is he? Anyone I know?"

Silently begging forgiveness from Papa Joe's ghost, Nicole plowed on. "You might know him. Do you remember Dante LaPalma?"

"Dante LaPalma. No, I don't think—"

Suddenly, the name must have registered. Rhoda's hand fluttered to her throat. Nicole could've sworn she heard ghostly laughter in her ears. Somewhere above them, Papa Joe was rolling on a cloud, holding his sides with glee at the stricken look on his ex-wife's face.

"Not Joe Corbet's grandson!" she exclaimed, her complexion whitening beneath her unsmeared maquillage.

In thirty years, Nicole had never seen anything or anyone ruffle Mother's feathers. Until now.

Hey, Dante, looks like I owe you one. Thanks!

"Why on earth would you waste your time with trash like that?" Rhoda demanded. "He's worse than his grandfather."

"How would you know what he's like?" Hands on hips, she hitched one leg forward. "When was the last time you saw Papa Joe, much less anyone related to him?"

"By *choice*, Nicole! That man was a loser twenty years ago. I can't imagine he's made anything of his life since then."

"Papa Joe was never a loser!"

Rhoda's eyes rolled like an angst-ridden teenager's. "I'm not talking about Joe. I'm speaking of Dante. I may not have seen Joe in years; but that doesn't mean I haven't run into one or two common acquaintances since our divorce. Joe doted on Dante. And in the end, that boy broke his heart."

To annoy her mother, she flashed a smirk full of innuendo. "Trust me. He's not a boy anymore."

"Maybe not, but trust *me*, you don't know the things about him that I know."

Folding her arms over her chest, Nicole glared, eyes burning with disbelief. "Like what?"

"Like he got into a lot of trouble as a kid. Barely scraped by the law more times than you can count. From what I heard, Dante LaPalma was one step above a juvenile delinquent." She pinched her fingers together. "One very small step."

"So what? He's grown out of his delinquent ways."

"Really? You think so? Did he tell you about his marriage? How he had to marry a girl when he was eighteen because he got her pregnant?" Triumph lit an unholy fire in her eyes. "What do you think of your Prince Charming now, hmmm?"

"Well, he's obviously fertile," she retorted. "Which should put your mind at ease about those grandchildren you're so eager to have."

Rhoda's complexion turned as purple as Nicole's blouse. "Mark my words, keep hanging around with that shady character and he'll ruin everything."

"What everything?"

"I'm talking about your life, Nicole. Your future. Leopards don't change their spots. He ruined that poor girl in Florida. He'll do the same to you."

"How do you know?" Nicole laughed. "That was . . . what? A dozen years ago? More? He was a teenager who made a mistake. And wonder of wonders, he owned up to it!"

"And when he tired of his wife and domestic life, he simply walked away."

Nicole's brain traveled at light speed to leap to Dante's defense. "Funny. According to Papa Joe, Dante still pays a lot of his ex-wife's expenses. I'd imagine he's fairly generous with his son as well."

"I suppose he is." Rhoda lifted her chin. "But I hardly think paying their bills makes him an ideal husband and father."

"Really? I know an adult parent who'd let her kid starve on the street, even though she has the means to do otherwise."

Zing! The barb hit home.

"Don't lash out at me for your shortsightedness. You're in

the real estate business, for God's sake. All you had to do was check out the deed and then plug the particulars into that Multiple Listing software you have in your office. Compare similar sales in the area. You would've known immediately how much this property was worth."

"You're absolutely right," Nicole admitted in a husky whisper. "It's my fault. I trusted you. But don't worry. I'll never make that mistake again."

"Save the melodrama for your shrink," Rhoda retorted. "I've waited years for you to grow up and move on with your life. And as long as you keep cloistering yourself in this house, you'll never realize your potential."

"Thanks, Mom. Thanks a lot."

Placing a hand on Nicole's shoulder, she softened her tone. "Believe it or not, I'm doing this for your own good. Even if you handed over the full market value tomorrow—in cash— I wouldn't sell this house to you. The day after your thirtieth birthday, you're out of here."

Chapter Seven

For the next three days, Nicole existed in an overactive beehive. No one could get close to her. Those who tried were quickly stung by her cranky attitude and sharp tongue. Nothing permeated her psyche over the high-pitched buzz of her mother's statement: *Even if you handed over the full market value tomorrow—in cash—I wouldn't sell this house to you.*

The words crushed her. She had nothing left now. No hope, no motivation, no reason to chase Papa Joe's silly treasure dream. Queen Rhoda had spoken.

Each night when she returned home from work, she wandered room to room, branding memories in her heart for the day she'd be forced to say good-bye forever. Girlish giggles echoed in the living room, along with the silly soundtracks of Saturday-morning cartoons. Odors of Sunday roasts and morning bacon infused the kitchen. In the attic, she rummaged through the chest of old toys, Barbie dolls, and stuffed animals for her Easy-Bake Oven. She remembered those mini cakes, baked by lightbulb, she'd fussed over for Papa Joe. They'd probably tasted like sawdust, but Papa Joe always ate every crumb, licked his lips, and proclaimed them the finest desserts he'd ever tasted.

During a humid Thursday sunset, she strolled the empty dock, but her mind saw her father seated beside a little blond girl, feet dangling over the edge as they hurled fishing lines into the shimmering water. Squeals of laughter rent the air when the child felt sharp tugs and, with Daddy's help, reeled in her first snapper.

Sobs choked Nicole's throat and she squeezed her eyes shut until the visions floated into mist. How could she leave this place? How could she ever be happy anywhere else? Without the memories that made up who she was? Why did her mother have to be so stubborn, so judgmental, so determined to make Nicole walk her line, or her aisle as it were?

Tears streaming down her cheeks, she raced up the path cutting through the dunes, past the piping plover nesting grounds to the house where that little blond girl had grown up. She stopped short when she spotted a slender woman, real, with dark hair and glossy teddy-bear eyes, waiting for her on the back stoop. Beside the woman sat a paper sack.

Nicole blinked. "Farrah?"

In reply, the woman reached into the sack and pulled out a pint of Ben & Jerry's New York Super Fudge Chunk ice cream.

"You haven't answered your phone in the last three days," her best friend said. "Figured you could use some of this."

Wiping away tears with the heel of her hand, Nicole offered a tremulous smile. "Come on inside. I'll get the spoons."

"So . . . ?" Farrah said in her best mock Jewish-mother tone. "What's new?"

Nicole looked up from the ice cream in front of her. "Rhoda's back in town."

"Now, *there's* a news flash," Farrah replied, waving her spoon. "Of course I would've liked to hear about it yesterday."

Embarrassment hit her behind the knees, and Nicole sank into the kitchen chair. "She went to see you?"

"Well, I'm not sure 'see me' is the right terminology for what Rhoda did. What made her come here now?"

"As best as I can figure, to fix me up with Dr. Danny. Apparently, he's divorced again."

Screwing up her face, Farrah shuddered violently. "Eeew!" Then she laughed. Like a loon.

"It's not *that* funny." Nicole scraped her spoon against the top layer of ice cream.

"Oh, come on," Farrah said between giggles. "If it had happened to me you'd be hysterical right now. Remember when my mother set me up with her hairdresser's son?"

Nicole nearly spat out the mouthful of chocolaty goodness. "That was priceless. Within five minutes of meeting you he told you he likes to wear women's underwear and it would never work out between you because he wore a different size panty."

"I'm glad you can still find amusement at my expense."

"Well, at least you found your Prince Charming at last. I'm still kissing frogs."

"So this Dante LaPalma's another frog?"

Clink! She dropped the spoon. "How did you know—" Before she finished the question, she knew the answer. "My mother."

"Yup," Farrah replied. "She came to the banquet hall and proceeded to suggest I have Jason introduce you to some of his business acquaintances. Said a 'real friend' would have found you someone to take your mind off 'that rascal' Dante LaPalma."

Oh. My. God. "She didn't."

"She did."

"What did you say?"

Farrah shrugged. "I was kind of at a disadvantage since I have no idea who Dante LaPalma is, but I rolled with it. Told her I had tried introducing you to several of my husband's acquaintances, but you still seemed to prefer disreputable men. I'm not sure which burned her butt more: my mentioning my *husband* or the fact you'd turned down a guy like Jack Carpenter for someone named Dante LaPalma. I didn't add I'd make the same choice based on name alone. And I *know* Jack." She swiped the container from Nicole, scooped out a spoonful of ice cream studded with a white chocolate square. "Of course, I've yet to hear a word about this Dante character. Which means I'm not leaving here until I have the complete 411."

Briefly, Nicole explained the details of Papa Joe's will, his relationship to Dante, and their skydiving adventure earlier in the week.

"You actually jumped out of a plane?" Brown eyes widened with admiration and disbelief.

"Several times. First in tandem with experienced instructors, and then just Dante and me. That's what Papa Joe wanted."

"Well, that explains your mother's visit to me. She would never approve you dating your Papa Joe's grandson."

"A: We're not dating," Nicole insisted. "We're trying to find the treasure Papa Joe left us."

"Uh-huh. Look who's become Cleopatra, queen of denial."

"There's ab-so-lute-ly nothing between Dante and me."

"If you say so," Farrah said, but her tone left no doubt she thought differently.

Nicole's eyes rolled toward the rust stain on the ceiling then to the ice-cream container before refocusing straight ahead. Sometimes Farrah's romantic nature saw things that didn't exist. "Whatever."

"Right. We'll just agree to disagree on that for the moment. So what's B in your list of arguments?"

"B: I'm out either way."

Farrah cocked her head. "What do you mean you're out?"

"Just what I said. I'm out. During her visit here, Mommie Dearest vowed no matter how much money I pay her, she won't let me have this house. The day after my thirtieth birthday, she's throwing me out. She claims she's doing it for my own good." She sighed, rose, and paced the pitted tile floor. "No matter what Papa Joe left me, it won't get me the only thing I want: this house. So what's the point in going on these brainless scavenger hunts?"

"For starters, because Papa Joe wanted you to. Second, if you don't accompany Dante on all these adventures, doesn't that screw him up? Wasn't that part of the deal? That you two had to do all these stunts *together*?"

With every question Farrah asked, Nicole shrank a little more. By the time she realized her decision impacted not only herself but Dante, she'd become about twelve inches tall.

"Yeah," she said on a sigh. "I guess I have to keep going, even if it means I don't get anything beneficial out of it."

"Well, there's beneficial and then there's *beneficial*. What's this Dante like? I barely remember Papa Joe. All I can picture in my head is a tall, skinny shadow with jet-black hair and a leather bomber jacket. And an endless supply of hugs."

"Picture a younger, broader version of that shadow and you've got a head start on Dante."

"I've got more than a head start," Farrah replied with another fit of giggles. "I've got a major crush."

"Ha." Nicole retorted flatly.

Farrah smirked. "Oh, lighten up. I'm just kidding. What exactly does Papa Joe say you're looking for?"

Nicole provided the details of the video and letters.

"This may sound silly," Farrah said, "but has it occurred to you Papa Joe might consider love the treasure?"

Nicole snorted. "Get bent."

"Okay, I admit, it sounds like one of my fairy-tales, but hear me out. Papa Joe described it as the greatest treasure in the world. Said you two should 'spend some time together and you might find something priceless.' What's more priceless than love? And how else do people fall in love than by spending time together?"

"Sweetie, you see love in two starfish floating together at the aquarium. Besides, do you honestly believe Papa Joe would make us jump through all these hoops just to date? Skydiving last week, surfing at Ditch Plains Beach this week. By next week, we'll probably wrestle alligators. The whole idea is ridiculous."

"Is it? Papa Joe adored you. Even if he hadn't said anything about you being the daughter of his old age, everybody knew how much he loved you. He obviously feels just as strongly about Dante. Now he's sending the two of you on these adventures *together*. Having you hold hands while you jump out of a plane *together*. Surfing *together*. Nine months from now you have to return to the attorney *together*."

Nicole's belly flip-flopped. Farrah had a point. Why did Papa Joe insist she go along with Dante on these excursions? To kill two birds with one stone. Two *love*birds? Was he simply trying to give both of them some romance?

No. She shook her head. There had to be more to this scavenger hunt. Didn't there?

Chapter Eight

A few miles from the tip of Long Island's fish-shaped tail, Ditch Plains Beach lay framed by high cliffs of beige and burgundy sand. About an hour after sunrise, life on this rugged beach woke slowly to a new day. Seagulls squawked while swooping over the surface of the Atlantic Ocean, seeking breakfast. Piping plovers zigged and zagged across the shoreline, their needlelike beaks poking holes in the sand to find minuscule marine worms and insects for their morning meal.

In the middle of this scene, Dante stood with Nicole and Long Island's oldest living hippie, gazing at the horizontal line where water met sky. Early morning sunlight shimmered like a sea of diamonds. Curling white waves crashed in a soft *whoosh* on the crystallized shore, washing his bare feet with brisk seawater.

"You're gonna love this place," Moondog said, stroking his

Grizzly Adams beard. "Just keep in mind there's a rocky ledge under those waves. Gotta watch yourself and don't overestimate the drag. You ever been surfing before, Dante?"

Dante stared at the rainbow row of boards, indulging memories of his rebellious teenage years. "Gramps taught me—despite my mother's objections."

Which raised the "odd quotient" on this particular requirement several dozen degrees.

"Wait a minute." Nicole held up a hand. "If you already know how to surf, what are we doing here?" She gestured toward the endless line of sand and ocean. "I thought this was supposed to teach us to keep our heads above water."

Dante shrugged. "My guess is Moondog and I are here to teach *you*."

Moondog flicked a silver cornrow over his shoulder, crackling agate beads enmeshed in the slender braid. "Your guess is one hundred percent correct. Today's all about Clipper."

Her complexion paled. "Excuse me." She turned toward the beach. "I just remembered I scheduled a root canal for this afternoon."

"Oh, no you don't." Dante gripped her arm before she could wade a single step. "We've got to follow Gramps' directions if we want to get our hands on that treasure. And we have to work together, remember?"

"Yeah, I remember," she muttered. "But I didn't know I'd be risking my life in some suicide mission."

Suicide mission? Was she kidding? All right, the skydiving had been a little hairy, but . . . surfing? Surfing was a kiddie ride compared to skydiving.

"Come on," he coaxed. "It'll be fun."

"Sure. Fun for you. You've been doing this for years. But me? At best, I'll wind up with nothing to show for all my efforts except a couple of broken bones."

Hoping to ease the building tension, he took a moment to scan her figure from bottom to top, radiating heat through his eyes. "And lovely bones they are."

"I am not amused." She gave the four words all the gravity of a queen demanding "Off with his head."

"Just keep the goal in mind. Remember the treasure. Hey, that's not bad. It could be our own battle cry. You know. When we jump out of planes, wrestle boa constrictors, get tattoos with dirty needles, we can shout out, 'Remember the treasure!' Think about it. A hundred years from now, kids'll be reading about our brave exploits in their history books."

Nothing. Not a snort, not a giggle, not even a smile. Apparently, charm wasn't going to win him points today. He hated to admit it, but he missed the snarkier Nicole, the one who chattered on about nonsense and took nothing seriously. The Nicole with him today was quiet, withdrawn, and sulky. She'd barely spoken to him from the time he'd picked her up at her house through the endless ride to the East End. When she did speak, everything came out in a monotone, without inflection or enthusiasm of any kind.

"What's up with you today?"

"Nothing."

Dante had gone through enough years of marriage to realize when a woman said "nothing" with that flat tone, she really meant "everything." He also knew that to dig it out of her was like picking at a scab: a painful, self-destructive behavior that would only leave him scarred and bleeding.

"Suit yourself," he said with a shrug. "Why don't you put on your wetsuit and we'll get started?"

Squeezed into a glow-in-the-dark yellow wetsuit, Nicole could barely exhale, and when she did she could have sworn she wheezed. Well, if she was going to look like an old school bus, she might as well sound like one too.

"You ever been snowboardin', Clipper?" Moondog asked.

She managed an oxygen-deprived "Sure," but didn't dare attempt a more verbose reply.

"Do you board goofy or natural?"

"Goofy."

"So you'll probably surf the same way. How about body surfing? Ever do that?"

"Yeah." In the confines of the tight suit, one-word answers were the best she could manage.

"Good. Then you already know the fundamentals of catching a wave and riding it in. That's half the battle. So, we're gonna start you riding a long board to catch waves. We'll paddle out beyond where they're breaking, like where those guys are."

He pointed at a circle of men and women, hands anchored to a multicolored chain of surfboards.

"Once we hit the whitewater, you can either plow through it or raise your chest up so's the water slips between you and your board. We'll work on other maneuvers like the turtle and the duck-dive if you decide you want to keep surfing. You and Dante can come back anytime, okay?"

Chances she'd return to this nightmare were as slim as note-book paper. Still, she gave him her brightest smile. "Okay, Moondog."

After all it wasn't his fault her mother had the emotional depth of warm Jell-O. Nor could she let Dante suffer for her mother's pettiness. So she'd press on, keep going, even if the victory would be hollow for her.

All she had to do was finish this surfing gig, get through whatever else Papa Joe demanded of them, and then use what-ever money she received to make a new normal life for herself. A normal life without her heart.

"Ready then?" Dante asked from her right.

Nicole nodded and climbed atop her board.

"Remember," Moondog said, "keep the nose a coupla inches out of the water."

She repositioned herself, and then gave Moondog a thumbs-up. "Got it."

At least, she thought she had it. Until the first wave pulled her beneath a powerful undertow. One minute, she balanced on her knees, prepared to meet the wave head-on; the next, an icy wall slammed her, and she fell.

Water filled her nose and mouth, sharp and salty. Her body became as frail as a rag doll's, and she somersaulted a dozen times, scraping her scalp against the ocean floor. Pain pierced from head to toes, cramping her legs. Water *whooshed* around her, in her ears to her brain. With no idea if her head faced the ocean's bottom or the surface, she panicked, fighting against the force crushing her from every direction. Her heartbeat thundered inside her skull, growing louder and more rapid.

I'm going to die. Oh, God, I'm going to die!

From the depths of the darkness, a strong arm wrapped around her waist, pulling her out of the maelstrom. She came up into sunlight and air, head aching, nostrils stinging, eyes burning, and her throat raw as she gasped for breath. With every scintilla of strength left in her fingers, she clung to the sinewy biceps that separated her from swirling death.

"Easy," Dante murmured, running a hand across her back in soothing circles. "I got you."

To her intense embarrassment, she broke into loud, life-affirming sobs. Dante only held her tighter while she humiliated herself for the benefit of the surfing audience.

"It's okay," he continued in that same comforting tone. "You got taken unawares. You're okay."

She pulled away, not because the fear subsided, but because his stroking affected her in far more dizzying ways. "I'm sorry," she rasped, her throat like sandpaper. "I can't do this."

"Sure you can," he replied. "You took a tumble, that's all. Happens to the best surfers."

She shook her head. "I'm done."

He chucked her under the chin, forcing her gaze onto his smiling face. With the sun gleaming behind him, he resembled some kind of water god, a delicious Neptune. "Come on now. 'Remember the treasure.' That's our battle cry. Right?"

Battle cry, schmattle cry. If today got any worse, those words would wind up her epitaph.

But what choice did she have? She couldn't let down Dante, couldn't let down Papa Joe. Regardless of her fears, she reached for the surfboard still tethered to her ankle and climbed aboard. Maybe if she drowned trying to get the money, her mother would regret her threat.

Every gray sky had some shaft of sunlight. If only she could find a way to give her mother that shaft . . .

Dante turned his car into the driveway and switched off the ignition. In the passenger seat, Nicole, head tilted against the window, slept the sleep of the truly exhausted. She'd put in a full day today with barely a complaint after that first mishap. And by the end of eight hours, she'd become a pretty decent surfer. Although when he'd told her, she'd only sighed, settled into the car, and stared out the window, silent.

At first, he assumed she was using the quiet time to work out the latest clue they'd received.

Sometimes you can't ride the wave to shore,
And you wind up beneath the sea.
But if you find something new that was old before,
Let the wave cast her spell, and she'll set you free.
A treasure awaits for the fun and the sport.
At last when the storm comes, you'll be cozy in port.

By the time they'd veered off Old Montauk Highway, however, she slept.

Now, pity pierced his conscience and warred with his sense of honor. He didn't have the heart to wake her. By rights, he should probably play gallant knight and carry her inside. But . . .

She had the keys to the house. He'd have to go through her purse, an offense his ex-wife insisted was punishable by death.

So now what should he do? He sat in the dark car, listening to her deep, even breathing. Finally, he gave her shoulder a quick shake. "Nicole?"

In her sleep, she sighed, a dreamy lilt. "Mmmm?"

"You're home. Can you get out of the car on your own, or do you want me to carry you?"

"Huh?" She jerked awake then, thrashed, and then slid up straight in the seat. "No, I'm awake."

Thank God. The way today had gone down, if he'd picked her up without her consent, she'd probably pound his chest like some sappy heroine in a bad black-and-white movie. Fay Wray to his King Kong.

Thankfully, she managed to climb out of the passenger seat. She climbed the four cement stairs, fingers white-knuckling the short wrought-iron railing all the way up.

After a couple of near misses, she inserted the key into the lock and then slammed her shoulder against the door. The recoil nearly brought her to her knees, but she managed to keep her balance, if not her dignity. The white coverall dress she'd tossed on over her swimsuit flipped up. Quickly, he reached a hand to return the dress' hem to a more proper position.

Nicole didn't seem to notice. With a loud series of clinks,

she tossed the keys onto the kitchen table. By the time he got inside and closed the door, she had sunk into the nearest chair and collapsed onto her folded arms. A whiny meow later, an enormous multicolored cat appeared and wound itself in and out of Dante's ankles.

"Hey, cat," he said. "Where'd you come from?"

"That's Bomber," Nicole murmured. "And no doubt, she just left the middle of my bed, where she's not supposed to be."

"Bomber?" The name took him a minute to recognize, but then inspiration lit up the dark corners of his brain. "As in the Bronx Bombers?"

She pointed a finger like a gun barrel. "You got it."

"Well, Bomber," he said, bending to run his hand from her ears to her tail. "You as thirsty as I am?"

The cat didn't answer, merely continued her live obstacle course while Dante did his best to maneuver to the refrigerator for some cold water. Jeez, the temperature had to be in the low nineties inside the house. He grabbed a bottle, unscrewed the cap, and gulped the chilled liquid with the enthusiasm of a man who'd spent the day in a blast furnace. Thirst quenched, he turned to offer a drink to Nicole and discovered her drowsing on her folded arm atop the kitchen table.

"Okay, my little surfer girl," he said with a sigh. "You win."

He placed the water bottle on the table, and then swerved her chair. Her neck craned at an odd angle, but she didn't wake.

Flexing his knees, he scooped her into his arms. "Bedtime for Malibu Barbie."

Heat radiated off her body, soaking his already sweaty chest. "Where's your room, sweetheart?"

"Down the hall, last door on the left," she murmured. One blue eye peeped open to glare at him. "Don't try anything. I've got a loaded gun under my bed, and I'm an excellent shot."

"Shut up and go to sleep," he replied.

In an effort to avoid Bomber's antics, he took long sweeping steps down the hall, conscious of brushing against the cat's spongy body. After a slow and awkward stroll, he reached an open door leading into a giant room of sugar. Everything was soft white: furnishings, carpet, walls, and linens. Sheer white curtains blew from open casement windows.

Three skylights lined up over the queen-sized bed and French doors allowed a full view of the sun sinking into the sand dunes behind the house. A gentle *whoosh*, waves breaking on the shore, provided a comforting lullaby. Obviously, Nicole found solace in this tiny corner of paradise.

Taking care not to wake her, he placed her atop the coverlet. Her head sank into the downy pillow with no protest. He slipped his arms out from under her and straightened. The wall across from him held scattered photographs, the only splashes of color in the entire room.

Well, well. What have we here?

Curious, he headed over for a closer look. The photos appeared to be arranged by subject. The first one to catch his eye, a wedding photo: a very young and imperfect yet pretty Rhoda with her cheek resting against her husband's. Nicole's father, no doubt. Dad had the same crooked smile as his daughter. The smile Dante liked to see light up her face. The smile he'd seen too little of today.

Frowning, he moved on to another series of photographs.

Nicole as a high school graduate, one arm wrapped around another graduate, a pretty, dark-haired girl with round brown eyes. That same girl appeared in dozens of photos, sometimes with an older couple, always with Nicole.

Along with the graduate photos, there were numerous shots of the two, apparently taken at various holidays. One showed the teenaged girls dressed as cats in black leotards with requisite ears and tails, carved pumpkins at their feet. Another posed them in front of a Christmas tree laden with ornaments and multicolored lights.

Their diverse settings included beaches, ballparks, the front car of a vicious lime green standup roller coaster, and the backseat of a white stretch limo on what could only be prom night. In the prom photo, the dark-haired girl wore a sparkly midnight blue flounce of a dress. Nicole sported a straight-cut strapless fuchsia number with a giant rhinestone heart in the center of her chest.

More recent photos showed both girls toasting with margaritas or cosmopolitans and, in one humorous snapshot, toasting by tossing real toast. Jeez, these two were major-league goofballs.

He moved on and came to a dead stop at a familiar face. Gramps, a much younger version than the old man Dante remembered, stood in the shadows of majestic pine trees, his faithful Harley Davidson Roadster leaning on its kickstand behind him, alongside a battered orange canoe. In this particular photo, Gramps had a wild afro of black hair, a fuzzy caterpillar mustache, and a very young Nicole, decked in a fringed black leather jacket and black jeans, held in his skinny arms. Weird to see the old man in such strange surroundings. But the final photo in the line took him by complete surprise.

Gramps again, this time standing beneath a palm tree, a sullen boy at his side. Both wore brightly colored swim trunks with splashes of red and white Hawaiian flowers. The child's face was shadowed beneath the expanse of leaves, but even so, Dante knew that boy well. How could he not recognize himself?

Amazing. She had a photo of him and didn't even know it.

"Brrr-oww."

The cat's cry snapped him from his reverie in time to see her black-and-brown-spattered tail disappear beneath the dust ruffle.

"Hey!" he whispered. "Get back here."

Dropping to his knees, he lifted the bed skirt in time to see Bomber scamper between the headboard and the wall, just out of his reach. His eyes scanned the rest of the floor beneath the bed, seeking something to wrangle the cat out of her hiding place, and locked on a large orange object. His hands closed around the hard plastic, and he pulled the thing out to get a better look.

A Soakmaster 5000, king of the pump-action water cannons. Instantly, his brain centered on Nicole's comment.

I've got a loaded gun under my bed, and I'm an excellent shot.

Stifling a laugh, he tilted the empty barrel. "You're out of ammunition, sweetheart," he whispered.

She must have heard him because she rolled over, opened

one eye, and said, "I suggest you put that back where you found it."

"Or?" he prompted.

"Or I shall order my attack cat to pounce on you."

He offered a mock shiver and sat down on the edge of the bed. Toying with the plastic gun, he nodded toward the wall of photographs. "Do you know you have a picture of me in your collection?"

"I didn't at first." She exhaled deeply. "But I figured it out after the will reading. Now put the weapon down and go home. I'm too tired to play anymore. I'll call you tomorrow and we'll talk about today's clue."

"'Til then, Sleeping Beauty," he said with a grand bow and left her room, and then her house, making sure the door locked behind him.

Only after he'd started his car did he realize he wouldn't be around to talk to Nicole tomorrow. Tomorrow he had a very special guest arriving at the airport: Gitan.

Chapter Nine

Nicole dreamed about Dante. Well, not at first. At first she dreamed she was a duck. A bright yellow duck, the shade and size of Big Bird. Spotting a crowd of ducks paddling in the ocean, she waded forward to join them. But the moment her webbed feet touched the water's surface, they transformed into bags of cement, pulling her deep into the murky depths.

She thrashed, but the water overpowered her. Seaweed tangled her arms and legs, hindering her efforts. She opened her mouth to scream and swallowed buckets of salty water. Just when exhaustion demanded she surrender, a pair of strong arms lifted her up into light.

"I got you," a deep baritone crooned in her ear.

Panicked, she clung to him, breathing in oxygen and the spicy scent of his aftershave. Never in her life had she smelled anything so comforting. Even when fear brought her to tears, he held her, rubbed her back and crooned, "I've got you."

Yep, he had her, all right. And she wouldn't mind if he kept her for life.

When she woke up, overheated and confused, her sheets tangled around her neck, she hugged her pillow to her chest while breathing in the scent of lavender fabric softener.

Dante paced the concourse in Islip's MacArthur Airport while waiting for Gitan to arrive.

Nerves pulsed and jumped like sparks off a car battery. He'd spent another sleepless night worrying about Gitan's upcoming visit. No matter how he tried to compartmentalize his worries, nothing—not Gramps' treasure hunt, not work, not even Nicole's laughter—took his mind off Gitan's arrival and the coming talk he dreaded.

A crowd of weary-looking travelers buzzed through a set of double doors, and Dante spotted Gitan's dark, curly hair above the swarm. Jeez, the kid had grown at least another foot in the last month! He wore the sullen look all teenagers mastered, along with black liner rimming his eyes, a black T-shirt emblazoned with the name of the current rock band cursing the Establishment, and a pair of faded black jeans.

Attitude rolled off him in waves. Hoo-boy. The kid didn't plan to make this visit easy on him, did he? Dante inhaled, and then exhaled his fears with the carbon dioxide. Pasting on a smile, he approached the throng. Time to get this show on the road.

"Gitan!" He waved to gain the boy's attention.

The boy gave a slight head bob in acknowledgment. Regret stung Dante, along with a wistful memory of a dark-haired child who, a few years ago, would've run the distance between them to close the gap faster. When had that happy little boy become such an angry young man? He should've cherished those days more.

The space separating them closed inch by inch. Dread of doing or saying the wrong thing paralyzed him, and he stood still as iron, waiting for Gitan to make the first move. For God's sake, he'd handled business deals with movie stars, multimillionaires, and spoiled rich kids without an ounce of the anxiety coursing through him now.

"Hey," the kid finally said with a nod.

Great. Awkward to the max.

"Hey yourself," he replied in a tone he hoped offered the right amount of affection. "How was your flight?"

Gitan shrugged, raising his backpack higher on his shoulders. "Okay, I guess."

He needed to find some common ground, something to help chip away the iceberg walled up between them. "You hungry?"

"A little."

"What are you in the mood for? Burgers? Pizza? Name your poison."

He shrugged again. "Whatever."

Jeez, would their conversations consist of one- and two-word answers all week?

"Hey," Dante said brightly. "I've got an idea. What if we head over to Planet Arcade? You can get whatever you want to eat, and then I'll kick your butt in Skee-ball."

Gitan's eyebrow lifted. "What am I, six?"

Six, nothing. They'd gone to Planet Arcade on Gitan's last visit four weeks ago, and the two of them had had a great time. What had changed?

"Okay, then, how about we get tattoos instead?"

"Funny." Gitan shuffled through the automatic doors leading out to the parking lot.

Disgusted with himself and Gitan, Dante sighed and strode out behind him.

"This is Dante. Leave a message."

Annoyed at getting his voice mail again, Nicole briefly considered driving to Dante's house to find out what was up. She'd already left two messages without receiving a call back. Where could he be on a Sunday afternoon?

Then sanity took over. He didn't owe her an explanation for his whereabouts. Okay, so she'd figured she would have heard from him by now. They had planned to work on the latest clue today. But he was a man, after all. And she'd learned to never rely on a man's promises. Even when romantically involved. Which, in this case, she wasn't.

So she'd work on the clue alone.

Find something new that was old before.

So . . . what was old? Chipped coffee mug in hand, she rose from the kitchen chair and laughed. In this house? What wasn't old? From the carpets to the furniture to the pictures on the wall, every lousy thing in this place was old. Not old enough to be considered antique, though. Just . . . old. Old and rickety like a weathered fence. Old and comfortable, like a favorite recliner. Old and familiar, like the photos in her bedroom.

Wait a minute. The photos. What had Dante said to her the night before? Cripes. Three cups of coffee and she still couldn't function at better than fifty percent.

Do you know you have a picture of me in your collection? Well, duh. Not just of Dante—of Dante and Papa Joe. Together.

Nicole only had two photos of Papa Joe, one taken with her and the other taken with Dante. Coincidence? No way. Papa Joe didn't believe in coincidences.

While striding the hall toward her room, she tried to remember how she came to possess those two particular photographs. The picture of her with Papa Joe . . . well, who knew, really? If memory served, she'd had it since soon after the shot was taken—at a picnic in the Pine Barrens region known as the Cathedral. Papa Joe had framed the photo and put it on her nightstand, so he could watch over her while she slept.

The second photo . . . Think, think, think . . .

She headed for the bedroom wall where the photos hung, her mind urging her to dig out the kernel in her brain's craw. When and how did she get hold of a picture of Papa Joe with Dante? Her mind flipped backward. She remembered the time as roughly five years after her mother had divorced Papa Joe. In one of their weekly phone conversations, he'd asked her what she looked like. Was her hair long or short? Did she still smile, even with the braces on her teeth? They'd agreed to exchange photos. She sent him a wallet size of her school picture for that year, and he'd sent this photo in return. Now the photo sat protected in a driftwood frame. But anyone who dared to pull it out would immediately see the dog-eared corners, the curled-up edge from where she'd stashed it in her jewelry box for so many years.

She stood before the two photos, thinking. Photos and her mother. The clue that sent them to Drop Zone Long Island dealt with a photo of Tina Louise and her mother's reaction. Did this clue have to do with Mother's opinion of Dante? Or of Papa Joe?

God, she hated this! She really needed a sounding board, someone to bounce ideas with her.

She needed Dante. Okay, so now what?

Before she could change her mind, she lifted the photos off the wall and cradled them in the crook of her arm. Time to take a drive. See where she ended up . . .

No matter what Dante suggested to Gitan, he met the same sullen look and apathetic shrug. They wound up grabbing burgers and fries from a fast-food joint along the highway. As they sat in a booth with their cardboard boxes and paper bags, Gitan connected earbuds to his MP3 player, popped them into place, and ate while bouncing his head to some drumbeat Dante couldn't hear. Thus ended any chance of conversation between them.

After lunch, Dante proposed they hit some balls at the local batting cages. Shrug. Fishing off the docks? Shrug. Any movies Gitan wanted to see? Shrug.

Finally, exasperated, Dante exclaimed, "How about I drive you back to the airport and you can sit there until your flight home takes off next week?"

Again, Gitan simply shrugged. "Whatever, dude."

Dante gripped the steering wheel tight enough to crack it. How was he supposed to reach this kid if they couldn't find any common ground? And when exactly had "dad" become "dude"?

Maybe he should try another tack. He thought back to his own teenage years. How had Gramps managed to keep the lines of communication open? Hmph. The same way he'd hog-tied Dante into jumping out of airplanes. Good old-fashioned manipulation.

With Gitan staring out the passenger window and no radio on, the silence soon become nearly deafening. At last, he thumped a hand on the dashboard. "Aw, Jeez!"

Gitan flinched and turned a steely eye in his direction.

"Sorry," he mumbled with feigned embarrassment. "I just remembered I have to stop by the garage. I might be a while. Do you want me to drop you off at the house first?"

For the briefest breath, the lonely boy inside the angry teenager broke the surface, and then just as quickly disappeared beneath the tide of adolescent angst. "No, that's okay. I'll go with you."

Bull's-eye. He bit back a smile. "Are you sure? I don't want to bore you."

"Whatever."

Teenspeak for, "Hooray, I'm going to work with Dad!"

With a set destination in mind, Dante relaxed while a much lighter silence filled the car.

Once inside Ironman's garage, he let Gitan wander while he headed upstairs to his office and turned on his desktop computer. As the tower hummed to life and the screen lit up, Dante strode to the plate-glass windows. From his perch above, he kept his gaze trained on the teenager in black one floor below who ran a fingertip along a chrome bumper, and then picked up a four-barrel carburetor for closer inspection.

"Dante?" A female voice called from the entranceway downstairs. "Are you here?"

His spine snapped to steel.

Nicole. How had she found him? He started down the stairs, but stopped in midstep when Gitan strolled toward her. On second thought, this first meeting oughta be good . . .

Gitan, all gangly attitude, faced off against Nicole who stood in the doorway, half inside and half out, arms laden with God knew what kind of paraphernalia.

"Hey," the teen greeted her with a terse nod.

"Hey," she replied in the same monotone. "Is Dante here?"

Gitan jerked his head toward the staircase. "Upstairs."

Instinctively, Dante took a step back into the shadows. He doubted either one of them would appreciate knowing he stood there, eavesdropping.

"Thanks."

Silence reigned. Well . . . good. Dante didn't want to be the only one who couldn't break through the kid's stone wall.

"I'm Nicole, by the way. Nicole Fleming. I'm a friend of . . . your dad's, I'm guessing?"

"Yeah," Gitan confirmed in his usual brusque style.

"You have his way with dialogue," she remarked.

Dante swallowed a snort.

She started up the metal stairs but only scaled two before Gitan called up to her. "Hey."

She paused and turned, one foot on the third step. "What?"

"Seriously. How'd you know he's my dad?"

"Lucky guess. He told me all about you. Besides, his car's the only one in the parking lot, and he's upstairs. That makes you either his son or a really quiet burglar."

"He did *not* tell you about me."

The hope in Gitan's tone surprised Dante. Surprised him enough that he wished he *had* told Nicole about the boy so she wouldn't have to lie on his behalf.

"Yeah, he did," she insisted. "I forget your name though. Sorry."

"Gitan."

"That's right." She slapped her forehead. "Duh. I remember now. 'Cuz when he told me, I thought, 'That's an awesome name.' You know? I mean, it's not a name you hear every day."

Dante's eyes nearly rolled into his brain. She must have realized she'd gone from friendly to doofus on the teen's approval scale because she sighed. "Anyway . . ."

Gitan, back to his normal, unapproachable self, replied with the standard, "Right. Whatever."

"Nice to meet you, Gitan." Nicole began her ascent again,

then stopped once more to toss over her shoulder, "Cool shirt, by the way. Did you get that at their last concert?"

Standing at the landing with one arm draped over the rail, Gitan looked down at the dripping bloody letters across his black T-shirt. When he looked up at Nicole, one eyebrow arched in skepticism. "You a fan?"

"Are you kidding?" She laughed. "I'm a *huge* fan. I have all their stuff. And I've seen them every time they've come to New York. I've got that same shirt, you know."

"No way."

"Way."

"Okay, then. What's your favorite song by them?"

" 'Ridin' the Razor.' "

Gitan slapped a hand through the air. "Get outta here. Girls don't like that song."

"Yeah, well, this girl does." Smiling, she spread her arms wide. " 'Your love cuts like glass' "—she sang with the ear-damaging tone of a high-speed drill—" 'Leaves my heart in the trash . . .' "

Gitan joined in on what Dante surmised was the chorus, but between the two of them he couldn't recognize a single syllable as English. After an excruciating few minutes of their tone-deaf sing-along, they broke into hoots and whoops.

"I can't believe you like that song," Gitan said, his voice tinged with admiration.

"So do I pass your test?"

He shrugged. "Maybe."

"Okay, then, how's this? You know that three-CD set they put out about two years ago?"

"*Three of a Kind*?"

"That's the one. Did you know it was originally supposed to be a four-CD set?"

"That's just urban legend," he retorted with a cluck of his tongue.

"Oh yeah? What if I told you I have a bootleg copy of *Four of a Kind* in my car right this minute?"

"I'd say you're full of crap."

She descended again, coming face-to-face with the dubious teen. "And I'd say you're not as smart as you look. Come on. Aren't you the least bit curious?"

The kid's posture went from slouched boredom to upright interest. "Okay. Maybe I believe you. So where'd you get it?"

Nicole switched her posture to slouched boredom. "My mother dated an executive from their record label a few years back."

"God, you are *so* lucky."

"Yeah, right." Sarcasm laced her words. "That's me. Lady Luck." She looked around the floor. "Hey, listen. Does your dad have a soda machine around here? I'm dying of thirst."

"Sure." He gestured for her to follow him toward the back room. "Come on."

Dante stood between the staircase landing and the doorway to his office, watching and shaking his head in amazement. Once again, Nicole had managed to surprise him. In less than five minutes she'd finagled more conversation out of Gitan than he had in two hours. She had him *singing* for God's sake!

Brrrring! The office phone demanded attention. Dante stood rooted, wondering what to do. Maybe if he left Gitan and Nicole alone for a while longer, her presence could break through the concrete in the kid's skull. Gitan might even take her into his confidence, tell her what had him so resentful, so bitter.

Maybe Dante himself should take Nicole into his confidence. Both men, the younger and the older, could use a buffer when they held their dreaded "talk." Nicole might play neutral party, taking neither side, just there for support . . . for both of them.

The phone continued to wail, drawing Dante to the desk. On the fourth ring, he grabbed the receiver, barked out the greeting "Ironman Motor Works," only to discover the person on the other end had dialed a wrong number. Just his luck. He really could have used a distraction.

He'd have to settle for some drafting on that Humvee order. The two people downstairs had no idea who'd called. Why not take advantage of the opportunity? Their camaraderie might make things a lot easier for him later. Maybe he should be grateful Nicole came along when she did.

Chapter Ten

So the goth wannabe oozing mega-attitude out of pimply pores was Dante's son. Not exactly what Nicole's vivid imagination had conjured. The way Rhoda had carried on she'd expected a cross between a street urchin from *Oliver Twist* and the creature that ripped the guy's stomach open in *Alien*.

This Gitan, though, she could handle. She'd sized him up quickly enough, recognized the pain behind a pair of stormy eyes. Just another kid screwed up by his parents' divorce.

Welcome to the club, pal.

They sat at a gray vinyl picnic table near a pair of humming vending machines. Between her hands she cradled a Diet Pepsi, and beside the icy bottle on her right lay the two framed photos and, thank God, a Snickers bar. A body needed fuel, after all. On her left sat her key ring, which she plucked up and dangled like a catnip toy for Bomber.

"If you wanna go out to my car, I'll let you listen to those CDs for a while."

Gitan reached for the keys, and she yanked them back at the last minute. "Hold it." She pointed a finger at his face. "No driving, okay? Not even doughnuts around the parking lot."

Tilting his head on one shoulder, he smirked. "Don't you trust me?"

"Not entirely." She tilted her head to match his. "Don't forget, I know your father. So promise me. You'll keep the car in Park at all times. In fact, I'll make you a deal. Leave the car stationary while you listen, and you can keep the CDs."

His dark eyes widened beneath the heavy black liner rimming them. "No bull?"

"No bull."

"Deal."

When she held out the keys again, he snatched them before she could pull back a second time. But he didn't race out. Instead, he laid the keys on the table and leaned toward her.

"I thought you wanted to listen—"

"In a minute. First, I gotta ask you something."

"Okay." She folded her hands. "Shoot."

"What exactly has my dad said about me?" While asking the question his slouched posture became rigid, as if preparing for a painful blow.

Her heart melted to goo.

Poor kid. For some reason, he needed a lot of validation. She shot a glance toward the office windows. Dante still hadn't deigned to make an entrance. Probably too busy playing with models, diagrams, and what-have-yous to worry about something as insignificant as his son's emotional well-being.

Empathy compelled her to lie—again.

"He talks about you all the time," she insisted with more enthusiasm than she felt. "Says he's really proud of you." She tried to remember all the platitudes she would've loved to hear from her own mother in her awkward teenage years. "He knows your life hasn't been easy since the divorce."

"Yeah, well, *someone* had to stay with my mother."

The boy's bitterness made her wince. How many times, in her youth, had she thought the same thing? How many nights had she envied those who'd escaped without another thought for Hurricane Rhoda or the daughter left behind? Still, she kept her tone light and shrugged with feigned nonchalance. "I bet your mom can't compare to mine."

His lips twisted in a grimace. "You're an *adult*. You don't have to live with your mother."

"Not now. But I did. For a long time." She unscrewed the cap on the Pepsi, which hissed carbonated euphoria into the air. Too bad the sound couldn't lighten the atmosphere inside the garage. "How old are you now?"

"Fifteen."

"Got any plans for college?"

He shrugged. "Dunno."

"Well, if you haven't thought about it yet, you should." Before he could offer a scathing comeback, she held up a hand. "I'm not lecturing you. I'm just giving you some friendly advice. If you decide to go to college, you can find a place far enough away where you won't need to live with your mom or your dad. Get a place of your own: a dorm, or share a house with some friends. Find out who you really are. College is only two years away."

The kid appeared thoughtful while he played palm hockey with the Pepsi cap. "Two and a half. Is that what you did? Moved out after high school graduation?"

The air around her chilled, and she wrapped herself in a pitiful hug. "I should have. I was too stubborn. Or too foolish. Or both. That's why I'm telling you. Don't make the same mistakes I did. I kept hoping I could get my mom to accept me for who I was. But all I did was prolong my own agony. She and I spent a lot of years butting heads. We still butt heads."

"Yeah?" His forehead puckered. "About what?"

"About everything. What I wear, how I look, what I do with my life. Mainly about men, though. We don't see eye to eye on dating practices."

"Your mom doesn't like my dad?"

"No, not really, but—" She stopped, realizing what he meant. "Wait. Back up. I'm not dating your dad. We're just friends."

He blew air out his pursed lips. "Figures."

"What figures?"

"Nothing." His eyes rolled like marbles. "So what does your mom do that ticks you off?"

"My mother divorced my father when I was four. Since then, I've had more 'uncles' and met more of Mom's 'special friends' than I can count."

"Your mom dated a lot of guys?"

"She not only dated a lot, she married a lot. She's on lucky husband number seven right now."

"Wow. That sucks." Gitan's dark brows knitted together in morose lines. "My mom's getting remarried in September."

"Ah."

That explained the waves of bitterness rolling off Gitan.

"I hate the guy," he whispered.

She propped her chin with one hand. "I'm guessing you've already tried telling her that?"

"Yeah. But she says I'm overreacting. Sometimes she claims I'm jealous because I'll have to share her with someone else. How stupid is that? Other times she tells me it's 'cuz I think if this guy wasn't in the picture, she and my dad might get back together." He snorted. "*Girls* think like that. It's been five years. If Dad hasn't come back to us by now, I know he never will. She just doesn't get it."

Tread lightly, kiddo. "What doesn't she get, Gitan?"

"The guy she's engaged to is a total sleaze. He treats her like a slave. He *hates* me—"

"Come on, Gitan. Curt's not that bad."

Dante's voice came from behind Nicole, and she jumped ten feet. Tension sparked around him, filling the garage with charges of static that tingled her skin. She glared at him, communicating enough impatience to make her mother proud.

Gee, look who finally decided to join the party.

As annoyed as Nicole was with him for taking so long to make an appearance, Gitan behaved in direct contrast. His expression went slack. All animation fled. His hands stilled, soda cap hockey forgotten. Nicole understood the switch to blasé as a defense mechanism.

"Whatever, dude."

"Stop calling me dude! I'm *not* one of your friends."

"Yeah, no kidding," the kid muttered.

"What?"

The static in the room heightened to fireworks intensity, and Nicole wanted to crawl out before she wound up burned in some bizarre backfire incident.

"You heard me," Gitan snapped, rising and grabbing Nicole's car keys in his fist. "I know you don't want to have anything to do with Mom anymore, but you could at least *pretend* to give a flip about me!"

Dante's eyes narrowed to slits. "You are out of line," he said through gritted teeth. "Sit down, and we'll discuss this—"

"Forget it," the teen cut in. "Just forget it."

He kicked the soda machine and stomped through the garage, his heavy black work boots thudding a furious rhythm.

"Where do you think you're going?" Dante demanded.

"Out." A shaft of sunlight glowed as the boy flung the door open, and then disappeared with a squealing slam.

Nicole took that as her cue. "Maybe I should just go home . . ."

Dante whirled on her then, face dark and forbidding as Satan's. "Why did you come here today anyway?"

"To work on the treasure hunt."

The saner part of her knew she'd regret wrangling with him in his present mood. But the impulsive, pull-no-punches Nicole had reached her boiling point. How dare he turn his anger on her? She'd only come here to help and what had happened? She'd wound up trying to reason with a sullen brat. And his son. If she'd wanted this much aggravation, she could've gone shopping with her mother.

Why did she put up with this ogre's attitude? For what? For some mysterious treasure probably more useless than a torn autographed picture of Tina Louise.

Slamming a palm on the table, she rose and gathered her photos, soda, and candy bar. "You know what? You're absolutely right. This treasure means jack to me. Especially now that I've lost the only thing I hoped to gain from it."

"What's that supposed to mean?"

Crickets invaded her insides, jumping and chirping. "Nothing. Forget I said anything. Forget I was even here."

Before she could sidle past him, he gripped her upper arm. "Oh no, you don't. I want to know what you two talked about. What did he say about me?"

Like father, like son. Didn't these two ever talk? Really talk?

She shrugged out of Dante's grasp. "If you want to know what Gitan said, ask Gitan. I'm not your personal liaison."

The moment the words left her mouth she wished she could take them back. Dante practically folded inside himself. His posture collapsed as he scrubbed a hand over his face. "I'm going crazy," he muttered behind his fingers. "I'm sorry."

"Forget it." All trace of anger dissipated like mist on a hot August afternoon. "I'm going home. Good luck with your son."

She started to follow the kid's lead out the door, forgoing

a similar kick to the vending machine. A pity really. She might have benefited from the violence of such an action.

"Gitan's not my son."

His whispered confession stopped her more effectively than a brick wall.

Nicole craned her neck to look back at him, her forehead puckered in lines. "Wait a minute. Back up. I'm confused. Gitan just told me—"

"Gitan doesn't know. In fact, very few people know the truth."

She faced the door again. "Let's keep it that way, okay?"

This time, he didn't attempt to stop her.

"There are parts of your personal life that don't concern me," she said airily. "Your son, or whoever he is, definitely falls under the category of NOMB."

"NOMB?"

"None of my business." She sprinted away as if the Prince of Darkness was on her heels.

"Gramps knew."

She halted, back stiff, but didn't turn around.

He could almost taste her hesitation. Time to take advantage of her indecision. "I think it's why he set me up on this treasure hunt with you."

"Why?"

He hid a smile. Nothing distracted a woman more than the need to understand a complex relationship, whether that relationship affected her directly or not.

"If you want answers, you have to stay and talk to me.

Now. I can't guarantee I'll feel so forthcoming about my personal life in the future."

"I'll take that chance."

He waited, saying nothing. She'd come around. She had to. He needed her to understand. He needed her advice.

The air dripped with expectation.

Finally, she sighed and dropped her junk-laden hands to her sides. "You're a real jerk sometimes. You know that?"

Breath he didn't know he held left his lungs in one long exhale.

"Come on," he coaxed, turning on the charm by offering her a self-deprecating grin and spreading his arms wide in invitation. "You're dying to know. Admit it."

She shook her head halfheartedly. "Your personal life doesn't concern me."

"Please? I need your help."

Ah, the magic words. Turning, she surrendered the fight, curiosity stamped on her face. "Okay. Fine. But only because I need you to focus on the treasure hunt."

"Is that the only reason?"

She shrugged. "Well, there's that. And because I really like your kid."

"What about me? Do you like me?"

Hands on her hips, she shifted her weight to one foot. "About as much as I like a steady dose of novocaine. You're a means to an end, pal. Nothing more."

"Liar."

Her cheeks pinkened, and he snorted in amusement. "If it

makes you feel any better, I like you too. Which I never expected to do."

"Oh?" She took the remaining few steps to the table with the enthusiasm of a dead man walking. "Why is that?"

"It's all part of the same convoluted story. But before I tell it, I'd better go check on Gitan."

She jerked her head toward the door. "Relax. He's in my car, listening to a set of rare bootleg CDs. He'll be occupied for about two hours."

"You gave him the keys to your car? Are you crazy?" Alarmed at the imagined destruction, Dante blasted off the bench with the speed of a moon shuttle. "How do you know he didn't peel out to go joyriding?"

"Trust me, he won't go anywhere."

"Yeah, sure, I'll bet."

"Relax. He can't drive so much as an inch without this." She dangled a tiny key from a Yankees medallion and chain.

He stared in confusion. "What is that?"

"The key to one of those club things that lock on the steering column."

"You actually have one of those?"

She shrugged. "Have to. The passenger door lock is broken. The door always looks like it's locked, but if a thief were to try the handle, he'd get right in."

"Why do you still drive that piece of junk?" He realized why the minute the words left his mouth. Saving money to buy her dream house. And he held up a hand. "Never mind. Leave the car here one of these days when you've got some time. I'll fix the lock. And anything else that's wrong."

"That's okay. You don't have to—"

"I want to, all right?" He spread his hands wide and stared up at the ceiling. "Would someone please cooperate with me today?"

"All right, all right. Take it easy." She spoke as if lulling a lunatic back to the asylum.

Taking a deep breath, he relaxed his attitude. "Tell you what. You help me with Gitan, and I'll fix your car door. Deal?"

She eyed him with suspicion. "I don't know."

"Please. I don't know what to do, and I'd like . . ." He paused, glanced at the concrete floor. Embarrassment threatened to swallow him whole. "That is, I'd appreciate your insight."

"On what? How to deal with a rebellious teen? I barely know the kid. Believe me, I'm the wrong one to give anyone insight on parenting. I can't even keep a houseplant thriving. Don't you think you should figure this out on your own? Without an outsider's help? He's *your* son, Dante."

"That's the point." At her blank look, he sighed. "It's a long story. But the upshot is that guy, Curt, who Gitan seems to dislike so intensely? Well, there's a reason he and Linda . . . that is, um, my ex-wife and I . . . well . . ." His tongue thickened, making the words nearly impossible to form.

"Dante, what?"

"Curt is Gitan's biological father." The sentence erupted as if from a tap turned on full force.

Her face turned ashen. "Curt? The same guy Gitan was just saying hates him and treats his mother like a slave?"

"Yeah, that would be him," Dante admitted slowly. "But I'm sure Gitan is overreacting. He's a teenager. Exaggeration is part of the uniform. Besides, he doesn't know the details."

"What details?"

He patted the bench beside him. "Have a seat and I'll try to explain."

She laid the objects on the table and then sat about two and a half feet away from the spot he'd indicated. Okay, so she was angry. On Gitan's behalf. He had to admire that.

What had she considered so earth-shatteringly important she'd tracked him down here in the garage? From the corner of his eye, he checked out her stash. The two photos of Gramps he remembered hanging in her room, a bottle of soda, and a chocolate bar.

"On your way to a tooth decay convention?"

She cradled the candy like a mama bear protecting her cub. "I haven't had lunch yet."

"My second guess."

She stared at him expectantly, and his muscles tensed from the jaw down.

Get it over with, coward . . .

One deep inhale, and he began reciting history. "I'd been dating Gitan's mother, Linda, about six months when she told me she was pregnant. In my head there was never any question the baby was mine. I mean, back then, what kid knew about DNA tests?" He shrugged. "I married her."

"How old were you?"

"Nineteen. Gramps tried to talk me out of it. But the more he pushed for me to be sure, the more I dug my heels in and insisted this was what I wanted."

"So what happened?"

"Seven years ago, Gitan was in a skateboarding accident. He needed a transfusion . . ."

The memories assailed him like shell shock. The nostril-stinging smells of antiseptic, the bright lights that seared straight into his brain, pea-green walls, Gitan's waxy pallor on the gurney, and the frantic speed of the doctors garbed in blue surgical gowns with masks. He blinked once, twice, a dozen times, until the hospital went out of focus and the walls of the garage reappeared before his eyes.

"That's when I learned I couldn't possibly be his father. Would you believe I actually argued with the doctors? Told them they'd screwed up and insisted they run the tests again. But I saw the truth on Linda's face."

"You mean, she knew?"

He squirmed under her shocked expression. "I'm sure she suspected. I mean, obviously there was always a chance I wasn't the boy's father. But the odds were pretty much split between Curt and me. And Curt . . . well, he wasn't exactly father material in those days. I was."

"That's just about the most diabolical thing I've ever heard."

He sighed. "Not really. She didn't do it out of spite. She was just a scared kid herself. I was already making decent money with Ironman in Florida. Curt was a high school dropout with a minor arrest record and a major drinking problem."

"Still. That's no excuse for sticking some guy with a responsibility that isn't his for eighteen years. I take it this bombshell was what blew your marriage apart."

"The marriage had fizzled a lot earlier, but I'd stayed for Gitan's sake."

For an excruciating minute she said nothing. She merely started at him, pity shining in her baby blues. "I'm really sorry, Dante."

He held up a hand. "Don't. That's not why I told you about this."

She slapped the table with both palms. "Well, then, why?"

Flinching at the urgency in her tone, he stared at the vending machines stacked against the wall. "Gitan doesn't know that Curt's his real father. Yet. Linda's kind of hoping I'll fill him in while he's here with me this week."

"Fill him in?" Disbelief laced her words. "Like you're handing down a recipe or something? You're going to tell him everything he's known about his life is a lie? And then what? You think he'll just transfer his affections from one father to another? What kind of twisted logic is that?"

Her umbrage confirmed his worst fears, yet offered him hope at the same time. Surely someone like Nicole, who had lived through far too many new dads in her lifetime, would help him ease Gitan's pain.

"Linda thinks once he knows the truth, he'll settle down to accept Curt without an argument."

"Like a robot?" She rolled her eyes and then clasped her

hands on the table. "Let me ask you something. How do you feel about what your ex-wife wants?"

He sighed. "I think the whole situation sucks, quite frankly."

"Then why are you involved in it? Why isn't his mother telling him the truth?"

"Because I'm an idiot," he admitted. "I volunteered to be the one to tell him. I figured I'd use more tact than Linda."

"You didn't want to look like the bad guy in the kid's eyes."

True. So he had no one else to blame for his current predicament. A heated flush crept up his throat. "I always thought Gitan and I were tight. But now . . ." The flush moved inside his throat, cutting off his airway, restricting his voicebox. "I'm not sure I even know the kid anymore."

"Well, you're barking up the wrong tree with me. I don't know the kid at all. So, go back. What exactly does any of this have to do with me, Papa Joe, and our treasure hunt?"

"When I first found out the truth, all I could think was I'd wasted some of my best years on a kid who wasn't mine." He picked up the photo of Gramps, grimaced. "It wasn't exactly my shining moment. And Gramps reminded me Gitan wasn't to blame for Linda's actions. Then he threw you in my face."

"Huh?" She blinked. "What do you mean?"

Eyes downcast, he shook his head. "You have no idea how much I resented you for years."

"You didn't even know me!"

"Not personally, but I knew all about you." Looking up, he offered her a sad smile. "There wasn't a person in Gramps' life who didn't know about the perfect Nicole Fleming."

"Me?" She flattened a hand over her heart. "Perfect? Now I know you're lying."

"Gramps really loved you. I think he aged a dozen years for every month he didn't hear from you. He worried constantly that your mother would somehow ruin you. He even checked with a few lawyers about finding a way to adopt you."

Her expression softened, and her lips trembled in a sad smile. "Really?"

Aw, jeez. The last thing he needed was a blubbering female. What happened to the healthy umbrage she'd simmered a few minutes ago? He had to get that Nicole back—the feisty one who'd rush to Gitan's defense.

"Yup." He leaned forward. "Think about it. If Gramps had found a lawyer willing to take his case, you might have grown up as my aunt."

The smile became an unhappy smirk. "Funny."

He resisted the urge to laugh, releasing relief in a shrug. "In any event, Gramps reminded me when I married Linda that I'd signed up for everything marriage meant: the good, the bad, and the ugly. 'Look at me and Nicole,' he told me. 'Just because I stopped loving the succubus doesn't mean I can forget about her daughter.' Gramps kept an eye on you out of love. I love Gitan. Really. I don't care that he's not mine. I want him in my life."

"You know what I think?" Nicole's soft voice reached through the fog of his misery.

Sometime during his confession, she'd sidled closer.

"I think," she continued, her tone mellow as butter on

hotcakes, "your grandfather was right. You're a very honorable guy, Dante. And I'm glad I have the chance to know you."

Leaning forward, she brushed her lips across his. Taken aback, he stiffened. Her kiss landed, light as a butterfly.

His arm encircled her waist, sliding her against him, hip to hip. He kissed her wholly. Not the winged peck she'd pressed on him, but a full frontal assault. She wrapped her arms around his neck and clung, the way she had when she'd taken her first tumble off the surfboard.

He'd been mindful of this moment from the first time he'd clapped eyes on her in the attorney's office. Since then, he'd burned up a lot of energy fighting the attraction, haunted by her laughter, struggling to dismiss her. All to no avail.

"Well, well." Gitan's voice ripped them apart with the sting of an elastic snap. "Maybe my dad's not as dumb as I thought."

Chapter Eleven

Nicole placed her hands on Dante's chest and shoved back. One sappy little story and she wound up kissing a guy she didn't even like.

Well, okay. Maybe she did like him. A little. Or maybe she suffered from chocolate withdrawal.

"Nicole said you two were just friends," Gitan reminded her with a wink.

The kid might not be related to Dante by blood, but both males seemed to have the inordinate ability to make her squirm with a look.

"Don't tell me you finished all four CDs already," she said to the teen.

"Nah," Gitan replied. "Your speakers are shot. The bass is all screwed up. Sounds like I'm listening underwater. Dad, if it's okay with you, can I pop these in your sound system upstairs? Then you guys can get back to . . . whatever it was you were doing."

Heat rocketed into her cheeks, and she unwrapped the candy bar to keep anyone from noticing how her hands shook.

"We were talking," Dante said through whitened lips. "And don't you think you should have asked Nicole before taking her property out of her car?"

"No." Gitan donned attitude-ridden adolescent armor, folding his arms over his chest. "She gave them to me."

"She did?" Dante shot her a look of surprise, or dismay, she couldn't really tell.

Nicole, mouth full of Snickers bar, chewed and swallowed. "I'm sorry. I probably should've checked with you before giving him a present. But I knew a true fan would appreciate them."

With a sigh, Dante waved a hand at Gitan. "Go on."

"Cool. Thanks, dude— er, Dad."

Flashing a grin wider than the ocean, he tossed Nicole her keys. They landed with a clink on the cement floor at her feet. While she bent to retrieve them, Gitan took the steps two at a time, the thick soles on his work boots thudding with the rhythm of a John Philip Sousa march.

"Just don't blow out *those* speakers, eh?" Dante called after him.

"Yeah, yeah."

Gitan closed the office door and within sixty seconds, the garage walls reverberated with the *thump-thump-thump* of heavy drums and bass guitar. One particular riff screeched like a dental drill hitting bone. Sucking air between her teeth,

Nicole managed to catch Dante's wince through narrowed eyes.

"Sorry," Nicole said when the music died to a low rumble. "I really am. If you want me to take the CDs back, I can probably come up with—"

"How can you listen to that noise?"

She couldn't help but smile at his parental outrage. "Why do you think I was so willing to part with such rare CDs? I don't listen to that stuff."

"But," he sputtered, "I heard you! You and Gitan were singing together. You knew every note of that song."

"I know enough about the band to bluff my way through a conversation with a fan," she said with a casual wave of the last bit of Snickers. "And the CDs are legit. My mother's old boyfriend really did produce them. That lent my bluff a little street cred. Which was all Gitan needed to connect with me."

"I'm impressed." He stroked his chin and then wagged his index finger. "You see. This is why I need your help."

"You still haven't explained what you want from me."

His eyes veered toward the closed office door above them, as if ascertaining Gitan remained out of earshot upstairs. Apparently satisfied, he returned his attention to her. "I'm not a hundred percent sure. Advice, for starters. I thought you might be able to tell me how best to tell Gitan the truth about his mother and me. I mean, you've been through a lot with your various stepfathers."

All of a sudden, a nagging urge to flee itched her feet. She *so* did not want to be there. "True." She kept her voice even while turmoil roiled inside her belly. "But I always knew who my father was. This is an entirely different situation than any-thing I've been through with the Ice Princess."

"Still. You managed to get Gitan talking about himself within minutes of meeting him."

"No, I didn't. I got him to talk about *you*. And his mother. That was easy. Since I'm not related to either of you, he sensed I wouldn't be judgmental. And of course, tossing in complaints about my own mother made him more secure about confiding in me."

"Which means he trusts you. So how about you stay with me when I tell him about Curt?"

She shook her head so hard her brain rattled. "No way. Nuh-uh. Not happening."

"Why not?"

"Because I don't belong there. Not for something so deeply personal. This should be between you and Gitan. With no out-siders. If I'm there, he'll feel the need to defend his mother to me, whether he wants to or not. He'll wind up hating me and resenting you. No freakin' way."

He sighed. "Can you at least give me some advice on how best to tell him? I'm at a loss here."

Some logical part of her insisted she stay far away from this mess. After all, getting involved would be more danger-ous than the undertow at Ditch Plains. The more she strug-gled to escape, the deeper she'd get sucked in.

But . . . Her gaze strayed to the office. That poor kid. And poor Dante stuck with the onerous task of telling the poor kid a virtual stranger was, in fact, his father. God, what a mess.

With those four words, sympathy beat out sanity. Again.

"For starters, don't wait."

She folded her hands on the table and gave Dante her sternest, most solemn expression. *Nicole Fleming, Girl Psychologist.*

"Tell him soon. Like ASAP soon. Give him time while he's still with you to digest all this and come to terms with it. I know you want to put off telling him until the last possible minute—"

"Gee, how'd you guess?" His sarcasm hit a nerve with her, but she smoothed the fine hairs on her neck with a quick swipe.

"Raw experience. My mom told me Dad was leaving seconds before I went to school one day. She saw the bus come around the corner, handed me my lunch, and said, 'By the way, honey. Daddy won't be here when you get home. He and I are splitting up.' That's how I found out about my parents' divorce."

Hissssss! He sucked breath as if she'd twisted a knife between his ribs. "Jeez. How did you survive with that woman?"

She shrugged. "I didn't exactly have a choice. I bet if she could've skipped the conversation entirely, she would have."

"Like you wouldn't notice your father wasn't home after a day or two?"

"Mom's very big on conducting life as 'business as usual.' She probably figured if I buried myself in ABCs and 123s, I wouldn't feel the pain. With Rhoda, avoidance is her ally."

"I'm sorry, Nicole. Really."

"Don't." She meant to tell him not to feel sorry for her, but the words blocked her throat and tears pricked her eyes. She sniffed them back, gulped, and changed gears. "Don't make the same mistake with Gitan. Don't wait 'til he's boarding his flight and then toss in the details of who his real father is at the last minute. He's going to need tons of support and time to sort through what you've told him. Give him all the help he needs to digest this. Answer his questions."

"Okay. I guess I can do that."

"Be honest but tactful. Don't make him choose sides. Remember, when he goes home he's going to have to live with his mother and this Curt character. Don't divide his loyalties."

"Anything else?"

"Yeah." The music screeched again, and she glanced up to see Gitan playing air guitar with furious head shakes and jumps around the office. "Good luck."

She gathered up the photos and stood, making a beeline for the door before she wound up sucked in deeper. Time to make a graceful exit. "Bye."

"Hey!" he called after her.

She turned.

"You never did tell me what you came here for. Did you figure out Gramps' clue?"

"Not yet," she replied and gestured to the upstairs office with a head jerk. "But it looks like I'll be working this one out on my own. You've got your hands full. I'll call you if I come up with anything."

Rising, he slipped his hands into his back pockets. "Wanna trade problems?"

"Not on your life, bucko." She laughed all the way out of the garage, into the parking lot, and only stopped when she settled in her car, turned on the ignition and felt her eardrums bleed at the volume setting Gitan had left on her sound system.

Dante watched her go, disappointed but resolved. *Don't wait,* she'd said. *Tell him ASAP* . . .

Problem was he'd never been much good at serious discussions with Gitan. He was Happy Fun Dad—the guy who took his son fishing or to ballgames. The closest they ever came to deep conversations was when they worked together on a vehicle restoration. Somehow, he knew this would be a lot harder than explaining schematics on a blueprint.

Slamming a palm on the table, he focused his attention on the Mustang sitting under a tarp in the third bay of the garage. Still . . .

Maybe . . .

If he could involve Gitan in a project . . .

With the first threads of an idea stitching the hole in his brain, he strode across the garage and up the stairs to pound on his office door.

A minute later, the music quieted, and Gitan poked his dark head out, annoyance oozing from his pores. "Come on, Dad," he whined. "It wasn't *that* loud."

"No, the music was fine," he lied. "I was just wondering if you wanted to help me with the Cobra for a while."

The kid's eyebrows rose in twin arcs. "Depends on what you're doing."

"A sound system." Dante forced a casual shrug. "A gift for some music guy. Wanna see what we've come up with so far?"

"Can I leave the CDs playing?"

Great. "Keep 'em low so we can talk over them, sure."

"I can do that."

Gitan stepped inside again, flicked off the pause button, and lowered the volume to jackhammer setting. Leaving the door open, he scaled the steps two at a time and came to a dead stop near the picnic table.

"Where's your girlfriend?"

"She's *not* my girlfriend."

The kid's eyebrows rose again, this time with enough doubt to make Dante squirm.

He'd have to explain Nicole's role in a little more detail. "She and I are working on a special project together."

"So . . . what?" His lips twisted to one side in a smirk. "She's like a coworker?"

"Yes, exactly."

"Funny, I've never seen you kiss Reynaldo or Jimmy before. They're coworkers, aren't they?"

Jeez, this kid didn't miss a trick, did he?

"Gimme a break." He headed to the Cobra, intent on hiding his embarrassment.

Gitan laughed. "Forget it, dude. I don't care who you kiss. I mean, I liked her."

"Well, good. I'm glad to hear it."

Because I like her too. More than I should.

Dante picked up a corner of the tarp, and then signaled Gitan to do the same. "One," he counted, "two, three!"

They flipped up the giant blue cloth, folding it in segments as they went along, until the entire car was revealed.

"Cool!" A wide-eyed Gitan strode around the Cobra, admiration growing as he took in the headlights shaped like strobes, the hood with the beginnings of a turntable set in place. "This is awesome, Dad."

"Thanks." Dante's wounded heart cracked. After tonight's conversation, would Gitan be so proud of him? Doubtful . . .

"You know, she reminded me of someone," Gitan said.

"Who reminded you of someone?"

"Nicole." He stared at the picnic table as if still seeing her seated there.

"Gramps maybe?" Dante suggested.

"Gramps?" Gitan whirled, eyes wide. "Why would she remind me of Gramps?"

"Because she's Gramps' stepdaughter." He opened the passenger door and slid inside to work underneath the dash.

"Man, we have one twisted family tree."

You have no idea.

"Speaking of that . . ." He started the dreaded conversation in a tone as matter-of-fact as if discussing the weather. "I've got something I have to tell you. It's about your mom and me."

"Yeah?"

Plucking the speaker wires, he separated the different colors. He couldn't look the kid in the eye. Not yet. "You remember when you hit that chain-link fence on your skateboard?"

The kid had the nerve to lift up one side of his T-shirt. "I still got the scar."

Even upside down, Dante felt the sucker punch to his gut when he stared at the jagged pink ridge running from Gitan's left hip to his groin.

"You were damn lucky. You could've died, you know."

Gitan crouched next to him, eyes rolling in the practiced look of teenage exasperation. "Is this gonna be another safety lecture? 'Cuz I don't need it. I wear my helmet and my pads every single time. Ask Mom. She'll tell you."

"No, that's not it. Though, I'm relieved to hear you learned your lesson." Gitan started to rise again, but Dante touched his knee, freezing him. He sat up and looked the boy in the eye, determined to do this right. "Your mom and I found out something while they were stitching you up that day."

"What? I'm adopted? I was switched at birth? Give it to me straight. I can take it." Gitan grinned, no doubt thinking this was some kind of joke.

God, Dante would sell his soul to not have to say the words aloud. But apparently, the devil wasn't in a bargaining mood. "Not quite. But . . ."

Get it over with.

His heart rose in his throat. "You know they asked your mother and me to donate blood for you, right?"

Gitan's reply came hesitantly, a hint of suspicion underlying the word. "Yeah . . . ?"

He swallowed hard. "We found out something that day . . ."

"You said that already."

"Yeah, I know I did."

Now. Tell him now. He raced through the words, hoping to abbreviate the pain, like ripping off a Band-Aid.

"I'm not your real father."

Face pale, Gitan sank to the cement floor and stared at him. "You're kidding, right?"

"No," he replied solemnly. "I'm not."

"This is a joke? Right? Because I said I could take it if you told me I was adopted . . ."

His heart rocketed up his throat yet again, and he shook his head. "It's true, Gitan." He reached out a hand, attempting to touch Gitan's arm. "I wish it wasn't but—"

"Shut up!" Gitan shot to his feet, whirling toward the wall. "Just shut up. Don't say anything else." Then, softer. "Give me a minute here, okay?"

"Okay."

Unsure what to do, Dante rose and stood a few feet away, allowing the kid to get his bearings.

His shoulders rose and fell with a dozen inhales and exhales. Time stood still. Neither spoke. Only the music played, ironically, the very song Gitan and Nicole had sung earlier.

Your love cuts like glass,
Leaves my heart in the trash . . .

Finally, Gitan broke the eerie serenade. "So who's . . . ?" The boy coughed, unable to finish the question.

"Curt."

"No freakin' way!" Gitan pounded his fist on the table, picked up a socket wrench, and flung it toward the vending machine. It hit the Pepsi emblem with a thud, then clattered to the floor. "No way! I hate that guy."

"Gitan, listen," Dante said, placing a hand on the boy's shoulder. "I know this is a big shock."

"Dude, you don't get it. I tried to tell you before. He treats Mom like she's his slave, has her running to fetch him stuff like he's some prince. It's always 'Run down to the store and get me cigarettes,' or 'I'm not eating that for dinner. Go get Chinese.' And she does!"

"I know you and he don't see eye to eye—"

"You don't know squat. You sit up here in New York, miles away from what I gotta live with every day."

He scooped up a hex bit, hurled it toward the same target as the wrench. A second hex bit followed the first, then a third, and a fourth.

Dante grabbed the kid's arm when he cocked back with a hammer in his grip. "Stop, okay? Stop. Let's sit and talk this out."

"Yeah, right. Now you want to talk. How about all the times I called you to tell you what living in that house was like?" He dropped the hammer on the table, leaving a chunky dent in the plastic.

"I'm sorry, Gitan. Really. But I'm listening now. Okay? So tell me. Talk to me."

"You really wanna know? Okay. Fine. I'll tell you. When I'm watching TV or playing video games, he walks by and smacks me in the head for no good reason. He goes through my stuff, looking for drugs. Meanwhile he's the one with rolling papers on the dresser. Mom says it's 'cuz he rolls his own cigarettes, but I'm not stupid. And now you tell me this guy's my father? My *real* father?"

"Hold up." Stunned, Dante clamped his hands on Gitan's wrists. "He hits you?"

"Yeah. Not hard or anything. Just a quick slap across the top of my head. Like it's his way of showing affection or something. You'd know that if you listened to me. But you're always too busy with your freakin' cars and your New York life."

The words stung like sleet, but Dante had more pressing concerns than some hurt feelings between the two of them. He gestured to the picnic table. "I'm listening now. And I want you to tell me everything that goes on in that house."

Chapter Twelve

Sunday night passed in a blur of questions with no answers. Nicole fell asleep sometime after midnight, the photos placed on the mattress beside her in the misguided hope she'd pick up something through osmosis. Unfortunately, the only thing she picked up was a dream that started with Dante running an ice cube down her bare, sun-baked back, and then went into realms best left unexplored.

At 9 A.M., a bleary-eyed Nicole headed off to work, still puzzling over her dream about Dante and Papa Joe's treasure quest. Why did Dante weave such a spell around her, whether she was awake or asleep? Okay, so he was a heckuva kisser. The man didn't only use his mouth to wreak havoc. He put his whole self into the art. He was the Babe Ruth of kissing. When his mouth fused to hers she heard the crack of the bat, saw the ball fly over the wall, felt the roar of the crowd . . .

Honk!

Shoot! She'd started fantasizing at a stop sign.

Not good, Nicole, my girl. Not good at all.

Managing to keep her eyes on the road and her thoughts off Dante's lips, she pulled into her parking spot and strode to the office of White Pine Realty.

"Wow," Chris Rudolph said when she opened the door. "You must have had *some* date last night."

"I wish," she mumbled and headed straight for the coffee pot in the back of the office.

Her favorite Yankees mug waited for fulfillment. She picked up the white ceramic cup with blue pinstripes and filled it to nearly overflowing. One packet of artificial sweetener later, she sipped and let the caffeine do its magic. *Ah, sweet mystery of life, at last I found you . . .*

"Okay, I'll bite." Chris leaned against the office's minifridge and scratched his ill-fitting toupee. "If it wasn't a hot date, what's got you looking like you've been chewed up and spit out today?"

"A scavenger hunt," she said and breezed past him to the receptionist's desk.

While sipping her coffee, she flipped through the pink slips of while-you-were-out messages, looking for questions about any of her properties in the pile. Nothing. Great. Her luck continued to run in the same direction. Toward disaster. And eviction.

A sigh of defeat escaped as she sat behind her desk and contemplated banging her head against the top until she fell unconscious.

"Come on, babe," Chris said. "Don't sweat it. Business will pick up for you soon. You know this industry runs in cycles. You're just in a dry spell."

"I passed 'dry' four months ago. Right now, I'm knee-deep in the dust bowl."

"So things can only get better."

She stared at him over the rim of her coffee mug. "Did you overdose on bad Chinese food this weekend? What's with all the fortune-cookie sayings?"

Before he could reply, the phone on his desk jangled and he pounced like a tiger on an injured mouse. "White Pine Realty, Chris Rudolph speaking. How can I make your homeowner's dreams come true today?"

The rehearsed speech Natasha insisted employees use when answering the phones made Nicole's teeth ache. Not to mention how physically challenged she felt, squeezing all that verbiage in on one breath.

"Oh, yes," Chris said to the caller, obviously having no difficulty with his spiel. "That's a wonderful property. Yes, it's still available." He quoted the current asking price, and then smiled at the caller's reaction. "Terrific. Why don't you come to our office? I'll pull the particulars for you in the meantime, and we can probably set up an appointment to view it within the hour." A pause. "Yes, we're on Main Street in the Village, at the corner of Gnarled Oak Road."

Cradling the receiver between his chin and shoulder, he flashed Nicole a thumbs-up.

In reply, she bared her teeth at him like a rabid dog.

He ignored her growls and kept talking to the fish on the

line, reeling the sucker in, inch by inch. "Absolutely. Just ask for Chris when you get here. And thanks for calling White Pine Realty." The minute the receiver landed back on the phone, Chris crowed to her, "Hoooooowwwwweeeee! Caught me a live one. Get this, Nic. A couple from Brooklyn, here on vacation and looking for their little slice of the American dream in the burbs. Saw that Cape Cod over on Tulip Lane and the wife fell in love at first sight. Husband says if it's as charming on the inside as it is on the outside, they're ready to put in an offer."

"Uh-huh," she said flatly. "Great."

In an attempt to forego more of Chris' boasting, Nicole turned to her computer and let her fingers fly over the keys to access the multiple listings.

Thank God he took the hint and wandered to the file cabinet. No doubt he was pulling "the particulars" on the Tulip Lane property for his soon-to-arrive clients. Not that she begrudged him this nibble. Chris had his own demons, including an ex-wife who had forced them into bankruptcy with her spending habits and twin prepubescent daughters doomed to follow in their mother's footsteps.

The bell jangled, announcing a customer's arrival, but Nicole didn't bother to look up. The couple from Brooklyn must really be psyched about that Cape on Tulip to pop over so fast. Where'd they call from? The deli around the corner?

"Nicole?"

At the sound of her name, she looked up and into the uncertain face of a familiar woman. Wonder of wonders. Despite her lie about an allergy to Freon, the wife of the couple from the week before had returned to her office.

Quickly she replaced the surprise resonating on her face with a warm smile. "Good morning! Mrs. Shanahan, right? What can I do for you today?"

The woman nodded and stepped toward Nicole's desk, purse clutched tightly against her abdomen. "I was wondering . . . that is, my husband and I talked it over and . . . would it be possible for me to see that three-bedroom townhouse again?"

Okay, so where were the hidden cameras? Chris said something about her slump changing and it happened minutes later? This had to be some bizarre episode of *Punk'd*. Any minute now, she expected Ashton Kutcher to pop up from behind a desk laughing like an idiot. Still, she gestured for Mrs. Shanahan to sit in the chair across from her.

"The three-bedroom?" Odd . . . She'd assumed they weren't interested in that property. Hadn't Mr. Shanahan remarked the space was too big for their needs? After, of course, wasting an hour wandering through it and checking all the appliances. Still, she wouldn't anger whatever god had placed this gift in her lap by questioning her good fortune. "You can absolutely see it again. Did you want to go right now?"

"Yes." Then she added, "If that's all right."

"Of course it's all right. We have the keys here in the office since the property is currently unoccupied." Nicole rose. "Let me just grab them and we can be on our way."

Mrs. Shanahan shot a hand out and clamped her wrist. "No, wait. Let me explain . . ."

Prying herself from the woman's clutch, Nicole sat again. "Sure. But it's really not necessary."

"Oh, but it is. You see"—she leaned forward, purse sitting in her lap and lowered her voice to a whisper—"I'm pregnant."

"Congratulations! That's wonderful."

Mrs. Shanahan blushed. "Thank you. We're very excited, but you see . . . we hadn't considered . . . You know my husband has a daughter from a previous marriage . . ."

"So you find yourself needing a third bedroom after all," Nicole finished for her, hoping to put her at ease. "And that yellow one in the townhouse would be a perfect nursery, wouldn't it?"

The woman beamed. "That's exactly what I was thinking. Gerry will make the final decision of course, but, well, ever since I found out about the baby, I've been thinking about that room. The way the sunlight filters in through the two windows . . ."

"Say no more." Nicole rose again. "Let me get the keys and we'll go take a look. Okay?"

"That'd be great." Mrs. Shanahan visibly relaxed. "Thank you so much."

Dante let Gitan sleep late on Monday morning. And while the kid slept, he sat in the still-dark living room, staring at the telephone. He'd kill for a cup of coffee, but figured the caffeine would make him too aggressive for the delicate task ahead. Later, with luck, he'd have a celebratory espresso. But first . . .

Picking up the handset, he dialed a familiar phone number in Florida.

Linda answered on the second ring. "Hello?"

Her voice was husky from sleep, but Dante didn't care if he woke her. Not while yesterday's conversation with Gitan still buzzed in his brain, as it had all night. Curt ought to thank God that a few thousand miles of highway separated them right now.

"It's Dante," he told her and waited.

He heard her sigh, a light rustle, no doubt of her sitting up in bed, and the strike of a match.

"What do you want?" she asked through obviously clenched lips.

"Still gotta have that morning nicotine fix, huh?"

"That's none of your business, Dante. Why don't you tell me why you feel the need to call me at—God—eight-thirty on a Monday? Did you tell Gitan about Curt?"

"I told him." *And got an earful in return.*

Tension built up inside him, straightening his posture to fighter's stance. In an effort to rid himself of the excess anger, he paced the living room.

Stay calm. Don't let her knock you off balance.

He needed Linda on his side and beginning this conversation with animosity would *not* be beneficial to his plan.

She exhaled. "Thank God that's over."

"Yeah, it must have been really hard on you." So much for keeping this conversation civil. Still, he'd double his efforts, try harder.

"It's way too early in the morning for your sarcasm, Dante. Unless you've got a point, I'm hanging up."

A lump rose in his throat and he swallowed it. "Would you be amenable to allowing Gitan to stay with me? For good?"

Since the day he'd discovered the truth, the idea of adoption had always floated in the back of his head. But now . . . Now, the idea became a need he couldn't deny.

She laughed, a hoarse sound that ended with a fit of dry hacking. "And what? Curt and I are just supposed to walk away? Let some *stranger* raise our son?"

"Come on, Linda. That's not fair. In Gitan's eyes, I'm less a stranger than Curt."

"He's *our* son, Dante. Mine and Curt's."

"Yeah, I know. But DNA tests aside, Curt better learn to keep his hands to himself."

"Oh, for God's sake, what did Gitan tell you now?"

"The truth."

"Or at least his version of it," she snapped. "He's angry, Dante. Angry and bitter. I'm getting married and he's jealous. Can't you see that?"

"Do you deny that Curt's hit him?"

"Once or twice when he mouthed off. And a light tap across the head when he's not paying attention."

Fury swirled, an anatomical twister wreaking havoc with his insides, but he kept a tight check on his emotions. "Are you saying that's okay with you?"

"Curt is his father," she replied in measured syllables. "He has a right to discipline the boy. And you have no say."

"Which is why I'm asking you to allow Gitan to live with me, rather than presenting you with an ultimatum." One deep breath and he plunged on, "I want to legally adopt him, Linda."

"Easy, Dante." The humorous lilt in her tone chilled his blood. "I can smell your desperation from here."

He said a silent prayer that Linda wouldn't pull a page from Rhoda's book and hold his greatest wish hostage against him.

For the first time in his life he understood why a parent might kidnap his own child. Because no way did he plan to send Gitan back to that house at the end of the month. Not after all he'd learned about what went on there: the verbal abuse, the smacks to the head, the drunken binges. According to Gitan, Curt was no better now than he had been before he became a guest of Florida's correctional system.

So now, if he had to grovel, beg, offer his ex-wife a limb, Dante would do it. Who cared if Gitan wasn't his by blood? They were related by years, by affection, by experiences they'd shared. And he couldn't—wouldn't—give him up.

"You think it's easy to raise a teenage boy?" Linda retorted. "I have half a mind to give you your wish, only so I can say 'I told you so' the first time he ticks you off and you call me to take him back. Which, I bet, would be less than a day after we made any kind of permanent arrangement. Gitan's not an angel, you know."

"That's why I'm willing to take him off your hands. Make it a temporary arrangement for now, if you like. With the idea we'll investigate the possibility of making it permanent at a later date."

"What? Like a lease with an option to buy?"

"Look at it this way." He struggled to keep his tone even,

conversational. "In one month's time you and Curt will be newlyweds. Do you really want a smart-aleck kid hanging around while you're trying to make a new home for yourselves? A new life? The life you always wanted? What do you think?"

"You know," Linda said thoughtfully, "Curt and I wanted to have a real honeymoon. Someplace like Hawaii. But we couldn't afford it."

"So what are you saying? I buy you a Hawaiian honeymoon, and you'll relinquish your rights where Gitan is concerned?"

Witch.

"Of course not," she replied, her tone sweeter than grenadine.

So . . . what? Now she's only half a witch?

"I'm only saying," she continued, "your generosity might make Curt more amenable to a discussion about the possibility of letting Gitan go. Call the honeymoon package a goodwill gesture on your part."

Gesture, my butt.

Still, he exhaled a long sigh. "I'll see what I can do."

"First class would be nice," she wheedled. "For a minimum of two weeks. With time spent on all the major islands. Oceanfront. Send me the itinerary when you have it. In the meantime, I'll talk to Curt about what's best for Gitan. Call me back once you've put together a package, and I'll let you know what we've decided."

Nicole had planned to allow Mrs. Shanahan as much time as she needed in the vacant townhouse. If it meant she'd finally break her losing streak, she'd have camped there all night with her prospective buyer.

Until the moment she stepped into the sunny townhouse at 35 Starfish Lane. Weird. She'd been inside this place dozens of times, and yet, today was different.

The minute Nicole opened the front door, this "fully up-dated townhouse with vaulted ceilings, natural stone fireplace, central AC, and expansive patio with views of the Long Island Sound" released tension she didn't know she'd carried in her shoulders.

As she stood in the terracotta-tiled foyer with its curved oaken staircase on the right and arched doorways to the kitchen, living room on the left, one word whispered through her.

Home.

This was what a home should feel like. Not like the ghost of bygone days. Not some shabby closet full of dusty memories. A home was a place to remember happy days of the past but also to anticipate happy days to come. Home was a promise— a promise of love.

These walls embraced her in a way her beach house never had.

Ridiculous. I'm just considering this house because the decor is so much nicer than the beach house.

Even before the thought fully popped into her head, she dismissed it. She saw lots of nice houses every day. And had for over a decade. None had ever affected her this way.

She actually imagined herself strolling down that lovely winding staircase every morning, headed for the kitchen where she'd enjoy her coffee and greet the sunrise from her deck. At night, after work, she'd kick off her shoes and settle in the cozy living room with a crackling fire in the winter and air-conditioning in the summer.

In the center of the living room wall, a sprawling bay window let in streams of sunlight. That, she considered, would be the perfect spot to display a massive Christmas tree every December.

She could picture the scene so clearly: a gorgeous balsam fir, at least eight feet tall, decorated with white lights and hand-crafted ornaments. Beneath the boughs, towers of packages wrapped in shiny paper waited to reveal their hidden treasures. She could smell her special spiced hot cider cooking in the kitchen. Her favorite holiday music played softly from her sound system placed in the perfect corner of the room to take advantage of the acoustics.

The idea hit her like lightning.

Nicole wasn't going to break her losing streak by selling this townhouse to the Shanahans.

Nicole was going to buy it. Thirty-five Starfish Lane was meant to be her home.

Chapter Thirteen

After finishing Mrs. Shanahan's tour of the townhouse, Nicole broke every rule of successful real estate agents. Rather than pushing for the sale, escorting the client to her office and beginning the paperwork, brokering for at least a binder on the property, she advised the newly pregnant woman to take her time.

"Discuss the pros and cons of the site with your husband," she suggested. "Look at other places. Make sure Thirty-five Starfish Lane is exactly where you want to make a home for yourselves and your family."

To her horror, the woman embraced her on the street outside White Pine Realty's office.

"Thank you for all your help," she exclaimed. "Gerry said all real estate agents were like leeches, only out for what they

138

could get, but you've been so incredibly patient and helpful with us."

When the woman broke the effusive hug, beaming, Nicole's conscience prayed the earth would crack open and swallow her. "You're welcome," she managed to murmur through a throat tight with guilt.

"We'll be in touch soon, I promise." Waving like the homecoming queen of the town's annual parade, Mrs. Shanahan practically skipped to her car.

Great, Nicole thought as she trudged inside. *Now what?* She really, really needed this sale. But she suddenly couldn't bear to part with that pretty townhouse and the promise it held for her.

What to do, what to do . . .

Her mind swam in a whirlpool of indecision. Sinking into the chair behind her desk, she waved off Chris' approach and then closed her eyes. What to do?

A light flipped on in the corner of her brain. Why not let fate make the decision for her?

For now, she'd do nothing. If the Shanahans came back to buy the place within the next week or two, she'd get the sale and hopefully break her losing streak. If not, once she'd completed this stupid treasure quest with Dante, if the townhouse was still available, she'd talk to Natasha about ownership.

Mind made up, Nicole refocused on Papa Joe's latest clue. She doodled the words on a dozen Post-it notes, tore the words into pieces and worked them like a jigsaw puzzle. Nothing came to mind. She scrambled the letters, seeking some kind of anagram. Nada. She Googled certain phrases. Zilch.

At home again and reclining on her fluffy white bed, she picked up the photo of Papa Joe at the Cathedral and stroked his outline with a fingertip. The Cathedral was a quaint area in the middle of Long Island's Pine Barren region, known for sky-high trees that formed a quiet canopy and a multitude of nature-based activities. Whatever the sport: mountain biking, hiking, horseback riding, or motocross, the Cathedral had acres of trails for a person to test his or her mettle.

Nicole hadn't visited the area in years, not since she'd picnicked there with Farrah's family when she was still in high school. Too many bittersweet memories whispered through those scrub pines for her. The Cathedral was also the home of the headwaters of Carmans River, a place she and Papa Joe frequented in the summer for scenic canoe trips. In fact, a canoe lay in the background of the photo she held.

Canoes . . . letting the wave cast a spell . . .

Was there a connection? There had to be. But what?

Think. Think like the old man.

An exhausted yawn stole her breath, and she laid her head on her pillow. Eyes closed, she tried to picture a series of squeaky wheels turning behind Papa Joe's crinkly forehead. But another man's face floated to the surface of her imagination. A man with dark flashing eyes that turned her insides to goo.

With an impatient growl, she rolled over and sank nose-first into the mattress.

Think. Think. Think.

Think "treasure." Treasure was normally buried. By pirates. Pirates who, in her favorite romance novels, looked a lot like a certain dark-haired man with a hellish first name . . .

Stop!

Okay, so what would pirates have to do with Carmans River? Time for a little more Google action.

Leaving the photos spread across her bed, she strode to the kitchen where her laptop lay plugged in and charging. Maybe she should charge her own batteries as well. A cup of coffee might clear the fog from her brain.

As the laptop booted up, Nicole filled the Mr. Coffee. Soon the invigorating aroma filled the air. Sometimes the mere smell of roasted Colombian beans stirred her intellectual juices. So while she waited for grounds to become beverage, she sat down at the computer and input "Pirates on Long Island" into her search engine.

She'd never considered suburban, mall-sprawled Long Island as a haven for pirates. At least, not the Jolly Roger flying, shiver-me-timbers kind of pirates. Software pirates, Wall Street pirates, robber baron pirates, sure. According to the Web sites she discovered, however, the area had a rich reputation for privateers, bootleggers, and shipwreckers from Jamaica Bay to Gardiner's Island. Approximately a fifty-mile stretch . . .

Great. So now what?

Mr. Coffee beeped, signaling he'd completed his brew cycle, and she stepped away from the table to retrieve a cup. Before she could return to the laptop, the phone rang.

"Hello?"

"Hey."

God, that sultry voice had her gripping the counter to keep from melting into the linoleum. Dante.

"Hey," she replied, faking nonchalance despite her sudden sensual haze. "How're you doing?"

"Okay."

Silence reigned. For a moment she thought the line had gone dead.

Then his breath hissed through the receiver in a deep sigh. "I told Gitan. Yesterday. After you left."

Her knees buckled again, but this time not from any romantic fantasy. That poor kid. How was he?

"And?" she prompted.

"And he's okay," Dante said.

Yeah, right. And I'm having George Clooney's baby.

"Define 'okay.'"

"Just okay. I mean, not great. This came as a real shock to him. He not only found out I'm not his biological father, but the guy marrying his mother—a guy he resents a lot—*is*."

"Wh-what did he say?"

"I think he was waiting for me to yell April Fool's or something. Then it sank in I wasn't joking, and he did some reconstruction to my garage walls with a few heavy tools. When I finally got him to calm down, we did some serious talking. I have a few concerns I'm addressing with his mother, but I'm hopeful that in the end he'll be in good hands."

Despite her brain's warnings to stay out of this mess, her heart wanted answers. "What do you mean? You and the ex are working out visitation?"

"More than that, but I can't discuss it right now. The upshot is I think he's gonna be okay."

Did he really think this situation would simply blow over so easily? Poor sap. One of these days he'd find himself plummeting to earth, this time without a parachute. But she swallowed the lump of discouragement before it could escape her lips.

"That's good, right?" she said instead.

"Are you kidding? It's great! But that's not why I called."

"No? Then why?"

"To . . . thank you. I don't think I could've . . . That is, your advice was spot-on. I could've screwed it up big time, but I didn't because of you . . ."

With those simple halting words, Dante, the fantasy pirate, stole her heart. Pleasure sparkled in her veins, transforming blood to champagne. "You're welcome."

The silence reasserted itself, and Nicole scrambled to fill the dead air with something, anything. Her gaze fell on the image filling her laptop: a drawing of William Kidd, upstanding citizen turned pirate.

"Hey!" she asked suddenly. "Did Papa Joe ever mention pirates to you?"

"The Pittsburgh baseball team?"

"No, the other kind. You know. Yo-ho-ho and a bottle of rum. Pirates. Maybe pirates who might have buried treasure somewhere on Long Island?"

"You're kidding, right? You think Gramps found some kind of pirate's booty buried somewhere and that's what this scavenger hunt is about? Aren't you taking the whole treasure aspect a little too far? I mean, you and I both know Gramps had a wicked sense of humor and a love for wild stories."

Okay, so maybe she was overreaching. But did he have to make her sound certifiable for voicing the possibility?

"It's an option, that's all. I don't see you coming up with theories."

"Oh, well, excuse me if I've had more pressing issues on my mind lately."

Ouch. He'd zinged her good with that one.

"You're right," she admitted on a sigh. "I'm playing around with different scenarios. I've got a stupid poem about letting the current take you where it may and the rest I'm winging. Maybe the photos have nothing to do with the poem. Maybe I'm so far off track, a GPS couldn't reroute me. But I'm trying. Okay? I know you've got a lot on your plate over there, but I'm not exactly footloose and fancy-free here either."

More silence. This time, Nicole was tempted to hang up. But she held on for a few minutes, scrolling through Web sites and tamping down the angry heat licking her cheeks.

Finally, he said, "Point taken. Now what? Are we digging up Fire Island?"

Her finger stopped rolling the mouse ball when she spotted two familiar words in a paragraph on Long Island Legends. "No."

With renewed interest, she scanned the story about a legendary pirate named Black Augustine who'd patrolled the Carmans River during the Revolutionary War, pillaging Tory households and wreaking havoc on British troops.

"No?" Dante's voice scattered the historical pictures dancing in her head. "What, then?"

"A picnic," she replied thoughtfully. "Complete with a scenic canoe ride down the Carmans River."

"Which is going to bring us another step closer to the treasure?"

"Maybe. When are you free to go? When does Gitan go home?"

"He's supposed to go back to Florida the end of August." The undercurrent in his tone suggested that date wasn't etched in stone. Was he hinting he could whisk the poor kid away if she requested it? Well, she wouldn't do that.

Although she really couldn't wait until the end of August. She needed to end this treasure hunt and get away from Dante before he permanently etched a home in her heart.

"We could bring Gitan with us," Dante suggested. "It's not like this is a date."

Caught in midswallow, Nicole sputtered on coffee. "A . . ." she coughed. "Did you say a date?"

"Yeah, the kid's got this idea that we're an item but don't want to admit it for some reason."

A date? With Dante? The idea held appeal, and that didn't sit well with her at the moment. She forced a laugh. "Why on earth would he think that?"

"Umm . . . may I remind you of the last time he saw us together?"

That kiss. Oh, God. That kiss still haunted her, brought her lips to puckering every time she remembered the taste of him, the feel of his arms around her waist . . .

"So, what's a good time for you?" His voice played easily into her daydream.

Her imagination took over, creating a hazy fantasy from some bygone days. Gliding down branch-draped waters at a lazy pace. Herself in a white dress, parasol shielding her face, a basket of delicious-smelling food at her feet. Dante seated across from her, bare-chested, muscles bulging with the exertion of the canoe paddles. While birds sang and Italian music played softly, she'd dangle a hand over the side to skim the water's tranquil surface. Just the two of them.

Screeeeeeech! Oh, yeah . . . just the two of them and a teenaged boy. A kid with a chip on his shoulder that rivaled Mount Rushmore. And he'd had that much attitude *before* he'd learned the truth about his father. Now, he'd probably tip the canoe with the weight of his resentment.

"Nicole?" Dante prompted. "You still there?"

"Huh? Umm . . . yeah. I'm . . . uh . . . checking my work schedule."

Right. Like she hadn't had the same schedule since starting at White Pine Realty back in 2002. Still, she took a few deep breaths, placed a hand over her heart to quiet the sudden rapid beats, and then asked, "How's Thursday for you?"

"Fine. One of the perks about being the owner; I can take a day off whenever I need to."

"Lucky you," she remarked.

"Yeah, well, rank has its privileges. Now, about the canoe reservation. Do you want to book it or should I?"

"I'll make the reservation. I'll put it under Papa Joe's name.

Maybe that'll trigger something somewhere and help us find whatever key we're looking for."

"And if canoeing has nothing to do with our quest?"

"Then we'll just try to have a good time, regardless," she replied. "Enjoy the scenery, have a picnic lunch."

Even if it's not a date.

"Fair enough. What should I do?"

"Meet me at Squassux Landing Marina on Thursday morning at eight. Bring a shovel."

In case I have to dig a hole to hide the fact that I'm falling for you . . .

Chuckling, Dante hung up the phone and turned to leave the office. The sight of Gitan lounging against the doorjamb stopped him cold.

"Hey." He nodded in Gitan's direction. "I thought you were rebuilding that four-barrel carb."

The kid shrugged. "I'm done. Came up to see if you wanted me to install it in the Cobra."

"Why don't you get started on it, and I'll join you in a few minutes?"

"Okay." Gitan turned, stopped, nodded toward the phone. "What's with the canoe reservation?"

How much of the conversation had he heard? Hopefully not enough to know they'd discussed him.

"Nothing," he replied. "Nicole and I thought it might be fun to paddle a canoe down Carmans River on Thursday. Whaddaya think?"

Gitan frowned. "No offense, dude, but I'll pass."

"Stop calling me dude."

"What would you like me to call you? I sure can't call you Dad anymore, can I? Some other guy has that title now."

Okay, so let's get into it. Again.

"What do you want to call me?"

The shrug returned. "I don't know."

Dante raked his fingers through his hair and drew breath in measured inhalations. He couldn't tell him about the conversation with Linda. Not yet. Too many variables hung in the balance and he didn't want to get the kid's hopes up.

"Look, I know this is awkward. But we'll work it all out, okay? I've already talked to your mother—"

"You did?" The kid's black-lined eyes widened. "You didn't tell her about the rolling papers I found in Curt's drawer, did you?"

"Relax." Dante leaned his hip against the desk. "What you and I discussed stays between us." More or less . . .

Gitan, gaze glued to the floor, shuffled his feet.

"You thought I was just going to walk away after being your dad for more than fifteen years?"

"You're not really my dad."

"Not by blood. So I can't give you a kidney if you ever need one. But you're still my son in every other way. I still intend to be part of your life." *And hopefully keep you here where you belong.* "Does that make it clearer for you?"

"Everything except what I should call you. I mean 'Dad' doesn't feel right now. 'Pop' makes you sound old. I can't just call you by your first name and I'm not throwing 'Uncle' in front of it. I've had enough pretend uncles . . ."

Picking up a drafting pencil, Dante toyed with the idea of jamming it into his ear. A quick, relatively painless death. Only one other option open at the moment.

"Okay, fine," he said at last. "You can call me dude until we come up with something more reasonable."

Or until Linda sees reason and lets the adoption go through without a hitch. If luck was on his side . . .

With a smart-aleck grin pasted on his face, Gitan flashed a thumbs-up. "I knew you'd come around."

"Yeah, yeah." Dante waved him off. "It's a temporary fix so don't get used to it. Come on. Let's install that carburetor."

Without another word, he strode down the stairs, Gitan in his wake.

When they reached the bay where the Cobra sat waiting, Gitan broke the silence. "You know, dude, I've been thinking."

Here we go again.

Cowardly as it might be, Dante ducked under the hood to fiddle with the manifold before asking, "About?"

"Nicole's car."

Dante swerved his neck to stare at Gitan in confusion. Nicole's car was the last thing he'd expected to hear. "Why would you be thinking about that?"

"'Cuz I sat in it yesterday," Gitan replied. "Do you know the passenger door doesn't lock?"

"She told me."

"And it's got a few dings too."

"Are you headed somewhere with this conversation?"

"Well, yeah." Again, the boy stared at his feet. "I was wondering . . ."

"Yeah?"

"I'd like to pay her back for the CDs she gave me. Maybe clean up her car a little bit and fix the door."

"I already promised I'd take care of the door."

"Well . . . can I do it? Maybe while you guys are on your canoe date?"

"It's not a date."

"Whatever, dude. Can I do it or not?"

He frowned. Why should he care if the kid wanted to do something special for Nicole? The fact that he *did* care annoyed him like a splinter in the thumb. "I kinda thought I'd fix her car next week."

Leaning one hand on the Mustang's front quarter panel, Gitan passed him a socket wrench. "Why? It'd be easier for me to do it while you're out with her. Tell her to meet you here, leave her car, and I can work on it while you're gone."

"What if you need help?"

"Reynaldo will be here. It's just a basic door repair and paint job. And maybe some new speakers."

He stopped, one hand gripping the socket wrench in midtwist, and looked up into Gitan's eager face. "Hold up, wait a sec. A paint job will take longer than one afternoon."

The kid shrugged. "So?"

"So, Nicole doesn't have the luxury to take a week off from work while you're beautifying her car. Did you consider that?"

"Lend her one of yours."

He blinked. "One of mine?"

"Dude, you've got *three* cars. And two motorcycles. You can't drive all of them every day. Lend her one."

Yeah, right. He returned his attention to the socket wrench and the bolt he was attempting to remove. "I don't lend out my cars to every customer that strolls into the shop."

"She's not a customer. She's your girlfriend."

"She's not my girlfriend."

"She should be. You like her. You wouldn't have kissed her if you didn't like her. She kissed you back, which means she likes you. So why isn't she your girlfriend?"

Oh, to be a teenager again. He hadn't reveled in the simplicity of those years when he had the chance. On a sigh, he replied, "It's complicated."

"Why? Is she married or something?"

"No."

"So then what's so complicated?"

"For God's sake, I barely know her," he sputtered.

"That kiss yesterday could've fooled me."

Exasperation finally got the better of him. "You know what? It's none of your business."

"You're right," Gitan said. "I mean, it's not like I'm your son or anything."

And suddenly they were back where they'd started.

Chapter Fourteen

By the time Thursday's sun rose, Nicole had considered, rejected, and reconsidered a dozen outfits, three different menus for the picnic lunch, and the plan to leave her car at Dante's shop so Gitan could "surprise" her with some improvements.

"Let him do it," Dante had pleaded when he'd sprung the idea on her Tuesday night. "He needs the distraction."

In other words, the kid wasn't taking the news about his father's true identity as "okay" as Dante had anticipated. And while she felt some sympathy for them both, she didn't quite think her sympathy spread to whatever Gitan planned to do to her car. Still, she relented. And then spent a restless night, her mind veering from the outfits hanging in her closet to the fried chicken and potato salad chilling in the fridge to visions of her faithful Honda painted black and purple with a skull and crossbones emblazoned on the hood.

In the morning she rose, showered, and changed her mind about her outfit again, finally settling on a pair of lightweight jeans, a tank, and a long-sleeved tailored shirt she could toss on if the air turned colder in the thicker wooded areas. She packed her soft cooler with the chicken and salad lunch, added several bottles of chilled water, and then headed out to the car.

Her heart cracked at the thought of leaving the Honda in an angry teenager's hands for several days, but Dante had promised Gitan would be under strict adult supervision and would do nothing outrageous.

"Minor improvements," he'd said. "He wants to take out some of the dings and fix your passenger door. Touch up the paint for you. That's about all."

"No joyriding?" she'd ventured.

"None."

As a show of good faith, he'd offered her one of his cars— apparently he had half a dozen of them lying around—but she turned him down. "You take me home tonight, and I can walk to work the rest of the week. The realty office is only a few blocks away, and the exercise will do me good. Besides, my boss makes me take the company car out with clients so it's not like I'll be majorly inconvenienced. As long as I have my baby back by Sunday night."

The deal was struck. She'd promised and wouldn't go back on that promise now. But if anything unexpected happened, she would be a very unhappy camper. After tossing the cooler onto the passenger seat, she slid behind the wheel and started the engine for what she hoped was not the last time.

She drove slowly, savoring the twenty-minute drive, stretching it out to thirty minutes before finally crawling into the parking lot of Ironman Motor Works. Her stomach flip-flopped when she saw the garage door yawing open like a giant brick monster ready to devour her car.

The urge to shift into reverse and peel out built to tidal-wave proportions. Then Dante strolled outside, and thoughts of fleeing took a backseat to a sudden inexplicable craving for dark chocolate. Six feet two inches of yummy, delectable goodness.

"Nicole!"

Gitan bounded out of the garage, waving her down, and obliterating her fantasy. He didn't stop until he leaned against the driver's door and poked his head inside. "I'll take it from here."

Yeah, right. Like she was going to let him anywhere near her car while the club thingie wasn't engaged. "Um . . . no. I'll drive it into the bay, thanks."

"I'm getting my learner's permit in two months, you know."

"Good." She gestured toward Dante. "Have your dad take you out in one of his cars when you're legal."

Shoot. She'd mentioned the D word. Based on the flood of color rising in his cheeks, Gitan had picked up on it as well. For a moment, they stared at each other, Nicole sorrier than if she'd peed on his shoe.

Then Gitan's pimply face broke into a grin. "Dude doesn't trust me, either."

If he thought she'd reconsider based on his confession, he was in for a rude surprise. She waved him off her driver's side door. "Why don't you direct me into the garage instead?"

He shook his head. "That's the problem with old folks. They don't give the younger generation enough credit."

"One more crack like that and I'll run you down."

Laughing, he walked toward the open garage door, headed for the back wall, and then faced her again, arms spread wide. "Come on, hit me. I dare you!"

He gestured for her to move the car forward, and she turned her gaze to shift into drive when a voice in her left ear nearly had her flooring the gas pedal.

"Why don't you let me do that?"

Gaining control of her overactive heartbeat, she turned to face Dante. "What's in a man's genetic makeup that has him convinced he's a better driver simply because he's a man?"

His grin would've weakened her knees if she'd been standing. "Actually," he said, his voice a husky murmur similar to a warm breeze on a Caribbean beach, "I was kinda hoping to scare the snot out of Gitan."

She laughed. "He's giving you trouble, huh?"

"Him and everyone connected with him."

"I'm sorry," she told him, but the smirk on her face probably marred her sincerity. She forced a somber expression and tried again. "Really."

"Uh-huh." He thumped his hand against the open window frame twice then backed away. "Go. Drive that sucker in. Then we'll start off on today's adventure."

Dappled sunlight shimmered the azure water around their craft from the moment they launched at Squassux Landing. Their canoe was, in actuality, a kayak. Long and sleek, the boat had circular holes for seating that forced them both to face forward while paddling. Relief coursed through Nicole when she discovered this best-case scenario. She might have wound up with her back against his chest or facing him and watching the sun's rays kiss his gorgeous face . . .

Ahem! Focus on today's outing and your research, Nicole.

Thankful he couldn't see her overheated state, she scrutinized the shoreline as they dipped their paddles in and out of the shining water in tandem rhythm. Papa Joe had always said calling the Carmans a "river" was an overstatement. At its widest, the waterway spanned fifteen feet, making it more like a creek in his estimation.

"Besides," he'd tell her, "these are some of the Island's best crabbing waters. And crabs don't live in rivers—unless they're uppity crabs."

But somehow she didn't think Papa Joe had sent her there for crabs that day. Problem was, she had no idea what to look for.

A gentle breeze kissed her cheeks and helped push the kayak in the right direction, so Nicole took advantage of nature's assistance. Certain they were well under way, she pulled her paddle out of the water to briefly rifle through her backpack. After finding the stack of papers she sought, she flipped through the notes she'd printed from her Google searches.

"The river is named for Thomas Carman, a sixteenth-century miller and purveyor of whaling supplies," she read to Dante's broad and straining back. "From the late-eighteenth to the early-nineteenth century, whaling boats landed here. Later, in the Prohibition years, the area was used to smuggle bootleg alcohol throughout Long Island and into New York City."

"None of which has anything to do with us or Gramps, as far as we know," Dante said, clipped and curt.

"As far as we know," she repeated on a sigh, settling the papers on her lap.

Allowing her mind to wander, Nicole gazed into the water. A snapping turtle popped up mere inches from her side. Tall, graceful birds, great white herons and snowy egrets, lined up along the shoreline, almost posing for a lucky nature photographer. How could she have forgotten such beauty existed so close to her home? If not for this treasure quest, would she have ever taken the opportunity to rediscover this paradise?

"Hey!" Dante called. "Are you a passenger or a participant on this journey?"

"Sorry." She stuffed the papers inside the sack and picked up her paddle again.

By the time they traveled into the Wertheim National Wildlife Refuge and floated under the Long Island Railroad bridge, Nicole had forgotten all about their treasure hunt and simply enjoyed the scenery. From there, she and Dante would travel to St. George's Manor where they'd have their lunch before reversing direction for the return to Squassux Landing.

"See anything yet?" Dante asked, drawing her attention back to the reason for their outing.

"I don't even know what I'm looking for."

"Well, that's helpful, isn't it?"

She'd seen razors with duller edges than this guy. When he was annoyed, every word sliced.

"I'm sorry," she muttered. "We should've done more research before undertaking this ride. I thought . . ." She groaned. "I don't know what I thought."

He craned his neck to glare at her. "You thought you'd make a reservation and some old coot would be waiting to tell us what to do next."

She shrugged. "Sounds stupid when you say it out loud, but that's how it's worked so far."

"Which means Gramps upped the stakes on us this round. Today's a complete waste of time."

Her heart sank to the bottom of the kayak. "Yeah, I'm beginning to think the same thing. I'm really sorry—"

"Forget it."

Yeah, sure. His words said "forget it," but his whole posture gave off an angrier attitude.

She scanned the treetops and spotted a family of deer lapping water on the shore. "Oh my God, look!"

"Mmm . . . terrific. Think they know where the treasure is?" He set his paddle aside and cupped a hand over his mouth. "Hey, Bambi, did Joe Corbet leave a message for us?"

Not surprisingly, the startled deer picked up their heads and fled into the thick underbrush.

"Guess not," he said and proceeded to plunge his paddle into the water again.

Tears stung her eyes. "I said I'm sorry. Obviously I made a mistake. Let's just enjoy the day, okay?"

Like a date. She didn't say the words aloud, but they hung around her like the heavy branches of the willow trees.

She had the bluest eyes he'd ever seen.

Dante sat across from Nicole, fighting to keep his admiration from riding ten stories high. Through all they'd done together—the skydiving, the surfing, and now this canoe ride—she'd given her all, never once complaining she might get dirty or muss her hair. In fact, right now she sported a smudge of dirt on one cheek. A couple of leaves lay scattered in her blond waves. Never once did she raise a hand to smooth or buff. Instead, she'd whipped open containers of fried chicken and potato salad and then tossed him a chilled bottle of water before grabbing one for herself.

Living with Linda had never prepared him for someone like Nicole. Not because she was lacking in the looks department. Nicole Fleming was downright beautiful. For some strange reason, though, she seemed completely oblivious to her charms.

Unlike his ex-wife, Nicole didn't worry about staining some obscure designer's outfit. She didn't play helpless to avoid breaking a nail.

This morning, she'd kicked off her sneakers and rolled up

her pants cuffs, wading into the water to help launch their craft. Only an hour ago, she'd repeated the procedure to drag the canoe up onto the beach here before lunch.

He could easily see why Gramps loved her so much, and maybe even why the old man had insisted they work together.

Nicole was a firecracker: all fun, sparks, and noise. Qualities missing in his life for way too long. What had Gramps said in his video?

She's one of the most joyful people I know . . .

Yeah. Dante could easily see that.

"Something wrong?"

Her question shook him out of his scrutiny in midscrute.

"No."

"You sure?" She cocked her head. "You look angry about something."

"I'm just disappointed we had no luck today."

Nicole's cheeks turned cherry pink, and she busied herself stowing the leftover food into their plastic storage containers. "I'm really sorry. I don't know what went wrong."

Guilt pierced needle-quick. Too much downtime here. While surfing and skydiving, adrenaline took over, leaving no room for anything but his heartbeat and the wind slapping his face. But here, everything conspired against him. The breeze, soft and warm, wafted her powdery scent to his nose. The quiet stillness on the river made him acutely aware of her breathing. The varying shades of blue in the water couldn't compete with the clear hue of her eyes. And the sunlight. The sunlight lit up her hair like a halo. Yet rather than make her appear some kind of fallen angel, the glints sparked impish fire.

He had to get away from her. As soon as possible. Before she made a permanent dent in his heart. He didn't have the time—or energy—for a relationship right now. Not when Gitan required most of his focus. Even this treasure hunt took too much out of him.

"Ready to start heading back?"

Her brows knitted. "I guess. I brought some fruit for dessert—melon and strawberries—but if you're in a rush . . ."

No strawberry could rival the plump ripeness of her lips. Oh, yeah, he was in a rush. "Sorry, but I'd rather not leave Gitan in someone else's hands for too long."

"Oh, sure. I understand."

But the unasked questions brimming in her eyes made it plain she couldn't possibly understand.

Chapter Fifteen

T wo and a half hours after lunch, Dante pulled into her driveway. "Home at last," he said and clicked open the lock on the car doors.

Gee, pal. In a hurry to get rid of me?

The afternoon might not have gone the way they'd expected, but they'd still had a good time. At least, she'd had a wonderful time—almost like a date, but without the pressure. So why didn't he ask to come inside?

Maybe he was waiting for her to extend an invitation?

"Would you like something to drink before you head out?"

"No thanks. I'd better get back to Gitan."

She hid her disappointment behind a wide yawn and slid out of the car. "I'm pretty beat anyway."

Murmuring a quick good-bye, she closed the door and then beat a hasty retreat. No way would she let him know his terse rejection stung. Tears blurred her vision, but she kept walking. Halfway up the drive, she pulled her keys from her pocket and found the one for her back door by the time she reached the porch. One quick twist of the knob and a push against the moisture-swollen wood brought her inside, where she immediately heard a familiar voice speaking from the front of the house.

Oh, dear Lord. Now what?

"The place hasn't been updated much in the last thirty years," her mother said. "But I think from a selling point of view, that's a plus."

What the—?

"I believe it's easier to interest a commercial developer in the property," Rhoda continued in that faux British accent she'd adopted while married to husband number four, the minor aristocrat from London. "You can knock down this building and the bathhouse out back and have plenty of room for winter water-view townhouses or apartments . . ."

Disappointment with Dante evaporated at this new onslaught. Nicole sped toward the living room and found her mother standing there with a woman she recognized from street signs in the neighborhood. Kim Camilo of Seaside Realty. Disbelief stopped her in her tracks, and she blinked, hoping her exhausted imagination had conjured these two before her. No such luck.

"Mom?" She hated the hesitancy in her voice, but couldn't squelch the angry tremors resonating from her heart out.

"Nicole, honey." Rhoda swept her into a hug with her usual aplomb. "I didn't expect you to be here."

"Obviously," she noted, backing out of her mother's embrace and folding her arms over her chest. "What's going on?"

"Kim and I—" Rhoda halted her explanation to pull the slender, dark-haired woman in the forest-green blazer forward. "You know Kim, don't you?"

"Yes, we've run into each other before."

"Of course we have," Kim replied in a tone sweet enough to make Nicole's teeth ache. "Real estate in White Pine Beach is a pretty incestuous business. We can't help but bump into each other now and again. How are you, Nicole?"

"How am I?" Nicole retorted. "Try confused. Or maybe outraged is a better word for it." Temper rising in infinite degrees, she whirled on her mother. "What exactly are you doing here?"

"Why, sweetheart," her mother said, voice smooth and cold as a skating rink's surface, "I've hired Kim to list the house, of course."

Rhoda couldn't have hurt her more if she'd stuck an ice pick through her brain.

"So let me get this straight," she managed through gritted teeth. "Not only do you plan to throw me out of my home, but you won't even allow me to handle the sale and gain the commission?"

Kim must have smelled blood in the air. She backed up several steps, inching her way toward the door. "Why don't I just snap some outdoor shots while the light's still good?"

She took off with a quick slap of the storm door.

Rhoda turned to the source of the noise and harrumphed. "Really, Nicole. You might have been a little more welcoming to Kim."

"Welcoming?" Nicole screeched. "Are you insane? She's here to sell my house out from under me."

"*My* house, darling," Rhoda corrected. "Don't forget. You're merely a renter. A renter served with notice that the house is about to be offered for sale. By law, you have to make these premises available for any agent or prospective buyer to view. You know that."

"And you know by law, you have to give me ample notice of any such viewing appointments," she shot back. "You can't just pop in whenever you feel like it. Whether you own the house or not, I'm entitled to maintain my privacy while the sales negotiations are happening."

"I assumed you weren't here," Rhoda replied. "Your car wasn't in the driveway."

"Not that it's any of your business, but I'm having work done to my car. That's all the more reason why you should've called first. You're lucky I wasn't home when you and Kim walked in here. I could've been in the living room. *Romantically involved with a man.* Wouldn't that have shocked Little Miss Incestuous Business?"

Rhoda waved a dismissive hand. "Please. Keep your fantasies to yourself, dear." She strolled through the living room and ran a finger over the mantle as if she'd become Chief Dust Inspector.

God, Nicole would offer half her bank account to get a

gorgeous hunk of man here right now. Just to shut her mother up. And not just any man, either. Dante. Oh, yeah. He'd be perfect. Not only would his presence set Rhoda's teeth on edge, he was also yummy enough to make Kim, the perfect realtor, envious. A win-win situation. Too bad her luck continued to run in the wrong direction.

"Tell me something, Mother," she said. "Did you purposely come here when my car wasn't in the drive, thinking I'd be out so you and Kim could rake over my possessions like vultures?"

Rhoda sighed. "I'm growing awfully tired of your histrionics."

An idea struck Nicole with the shock of a stripped electrical cord. "Louis isn't at a conference in the city, is he? You purposely came up here to start sale proceedings on the house, didn't you?"

"Yes, dear. I'm the villainess in your little drama. I'm not only responsible for your misery, I, alone, have orchestrated the global-warming crisis, the fall of communism in the Soviet Union, and killer bees. In fact, Walt Disney used me as his inspiration for the Wicked Stepmother in *Snow White*."

Once again Mommie Dearest managed to translate Nicole's valid arguments into childish nonsense. But this time, Nicole wouldn't let her get away with it. She refused to revert to type.

"Now who's resorting to histrionics?" she asked. Keeping a deceptive calm to her tone, she added, "Is it too much to ask that you might have consulted me about listing the house?"

"Of course it is. Letting you represent the sale of a house

you so obviously don't want to sell would be a conflict of interest. You might try to over- or underassess the property to satisfy your own wants."

That's it, Mom. Twist the ice pick in my brain, why don't you?

"Character assassination aside, you still could've asked someone in my office to represent the sale. At least allow my boss to gain the commission."

"And I still wouldn't have known if I was getting fair market value on the property. No, dealing with a stranger is much better in this case. Your father taught me early in our marriage that love and business don't mix."

Ouch.

In that single instant, Nicole understood her mother in a way she never had before. And her sudden realization drained the fight out of her. "You know," she said, her tone deadly soft, "I've always seen this house as a symbol of happier times. But you don't, do you? For you, this house represents the one time a man took you by surprise. Because unlike all the others, Daddy left you. Left us. That's why you don't want me to have it."

For an instant Rhoda's eyes widened, but the surprise quickly faded behind her normal icy facade. "Spare me your beach house psychology, Nicole."

"You can't bear remembering what happened here. And because Daddy left you, you expect me to do the same one day."

"I don't plan to stand here and listen to this."

"You've been keeping me at arm's length for years to

protect yourself from that eventuality. But you know what, Mom? If you hadn't tried so hard to hate me, we might have had a pretty good relationship."

"I do not hate you."

"Maybe not, but you tried really hard not to love me. Think about it. We might have been able to talk without having every discussion descend into a heated debate. But no. You had to protect yourself. From men, from relationships, from *me*. So guess what? I'm done. You win. Give me an hour to get a few things together and a day or two to put the rest in storage. After that, the house is yours."

"At last, you're finally thinking like an adult!"

"Yeah," she muttered as she headed down the hall to find a suitcase. "Yippee."

The tears she'd held in check with Dante were a gob of spit compared to the flood running down her cheeks now. But she wouldn't change her mind. No matter how painful her decision.

In the solitude of her bedroom, she picked up the phone and dialed Farrah's home number. Jason answered on the third ring.

"It's me," she croaked out. "Can I talk to Farrah?"

"She's still at work," Jason said. "Anything I can help you with, kiddo?"

Nicole promptly burst into wailing, but managed to give him the gist of the past hour's events through the watershed.

"Stay there," he said when she'd trailed off into a fit of hiccups. "I'll come get you."

* * *

Dante got as far as the highway before the memory of Nicole's stricken face guilted him into changing his mind. What was wrong with him? He was a grown man, not some hormonal teen who couldn't handle himself around the opposite sex. Nicole deserved better from him than a drop-and-run.

Once he'd pulled the car onto the shoulder, he grabbed his cell phone, punched in the number to the shop, and waited for one of the mechanics to pick up.

"Ironman Motor Works."

"Reynaldo," Dante said in greeting. "How's Gitan doing?"

"Good. We managed to get most of the dings out and put a coat of primer on the Honda. Never seen him work so hard before. I think the kid's got a crush on your girl."

Dante didn't bother to correct him regarding his relationship with Nicole. If he were honest with himself, he'd admit he didn't know where they stood.

Maybe he should find out.

"Okay if I stick around here for a while?"

"Yeah, sure," Reynaldo replied. "Gitan's in no hurry to go home. Neither am I."

"Thanks. I owe you."

He flipped the phone closed, then popped a U-turn. A quick detour at a nearby liquor store for a bottle of chilled Chardonnay and a short drive later, he paused at the crossroads for her street. On the opposite side of the road, a mint green Jaguar pulled a rolling stop, and then cut left in front of him.

"What the—?" He turned right and followed the idiot in the Jag.

Seconds later, the Jaguar sped up and into Nicole's driveway where it slammed to a halt.

Well, now this is getting interesting . . .

Curiosity burning, Dante pulled over a few houses away and cut the engine.

A man, tall as Dante but not as broad, stepped from the Jaguar. A speeding Nicole launched herself from the back porch into his open arms.

Okay, so who was this clown? And how long should he wait before punching his lights out?

The intense expressions on both their faces drove a spike through Dante's chest, and he rolled down the window to hear their conversation, but had parked too far away to discern their low voices. When the clown stroked Nicole's hair and she buried her face in the crook of his neck, Dante's hands clenched the steering wheel with enough force to strangle it.

Meanwhile, still wrapped around each other, the couple ambled up the steps and into the house.

Now what? A sane voice told him to turn around and go home. One love triangle in a lifetime was more than enough. No way would he go through that misery again.

Shifting in his seat, he reached to turn on the ignition when the two exited the house again. The clown held two suitcases, and Nicole toted a red plaid box that he guessed was a pet carrier. With her shoulders hunched and her eyes staring at the ground, she had the posture of a beaten woman.

Leaning over the dashboard, Dante squinted and peered harder through the windshield. Hard to tell from this distance, but she sure didn't look happy.

Okay, pal. All bets are off if you're making her cry.

Before his saner side could talk sense into his furious side, he opened the car door and stepped out. Fists clenched and ready for action, he strode forward, prepared to pummel the guy into a bloody pulp his own mother wouldn't recognize. As he drew nearer, their conversation grew clearer. The guy had a namby-pamby voice some might describe as "cultured." Dante preferred "snotty."

". . . Unless you need a drink or anything to settle your nerves first," the guy said.

"No, thanks," Nicole said, her tone flat and emotionless. "I just want to hit the sheets."

With this guy? Was she kidding?

"Don't sell yourself short, Nic," Dante called, sarcasm sharpening the words. "Hold out for dinner at least."

She stopped abruptly and stared, open-mouthed. "Dante? What are you doing here?"

"I changed my mind. Thought I might like to spend a little more time with you before I went home." His cold gaze took in the clown. "I didn't realize you'd get so desperate for a man you'd order one from Schmucks 'R' Us."

The clown had the nerve to laugh.

Nicole, on the other hand, shot red-hot lasers through her eyes. "What's that supposed to mean?"

"I think it means he's jealous," the clown replied. "A girl like Nicole doesn't sit home alone for long, Mr . . ."

"LaPalma," he replied through gritted teeth.

"Mr. LaPalma. As a matter of fact, I suppose I should let you know that Nicole spends quite a lot of time with me." He flashed Dante a snakelike smirk. "In my house. In my bedroom."

"Jason!" Nicole shouted, placing the cat carrier at her feet. "Stop it! You're not funny."

The clown turned toward her, innocence etched on his finely chiseled features. "What? I'm only telling him the truth."

"You're twisting it," she retorted. "Deliberately. Keep it up and I'll tell Farrah."

His laughter grew loud enough to shake the trees. "Okay, fine. You win. I'll just put these in the car while you calm the savage beast." Hitching the suitcases up, he jerked his head in Dante's direction. "Mr. LaPalma. Nice to meet you."

"Yeah, right," Dante replied, barely able to repress the urge to punch the guy square in the face.

"Are you out of your mind?" Nicole shouted. "Jason is Farrah's husband. There's nothing romantic between us."

"There could be," Jason singsonged from the trunk of the Jag.

"You're not helping," she singsonged back, and then returned her attention to Dante. "He's harmless. Really. It's a long story. I was upset and called Farrah. She's still at work so Jason showed up to help me out."

"Yeah, well, you're not riding in a car with him. He drives like an idiot. He nearly got us both killed at the intersection back there."

"Oh, please. I blew the stop sign," Jason said from behind him. "So sue me. I was in a rush to reach our girl." He sidled up to Nicole and draped his arm across her shoulder. "Come on, sweetheart. Let's get you settled. Mr. LaPalma, you're welcome to follow along. Nicole can tell you the whole story when we get to my house."

"No." He grabbed Nicole's wrist and tugged her out of Jason's hold. "She can tell me on the way. I'll drive her."

Jason looked ready to argue, but Bomber chose that moment to meow her frustration at being penned. Jason dropped his gaze to the carrier, then looked up at Dante, grinning. "Okay. But if you're taking Nicole, you take the cat too."

"Oh, no. *You* take the cat."

"No way. It's a package deal. You think I want to listen to that thing howl all the way back to my house? Forget it. We're not splitting up the set."

"Hell-o?" Nicole interjected. "I'm standing right here. Could you stop talking about me like I'm the dotty old auntie no one wants? Bomber and I will ride with Dante. We have a few things to talk about anyway."

"Sounds good to me," Jason said.

Yeah, sure it did. Bomber was caterwauling and lucky Jason had just danced out of putting up with the noise for however long the drive would take.

"But, Dante?" he added. "Let me give you fair warning. Nicole's been through enough today. You hurt her and—"

"And what?" Dante straightened to full height, fists at the ready. "Are you planning to take me on?"

"Me?" Jason gave a mock shiver. "God, no. I'm a lover, not a fighter. My wife, on the other hand, will destroy you."

Chapter Sixteen

For the second time in one day, Nicole sat in the passenger seat of Dante's BMW. This time, though, she kept her gaze pinned out the window, her posture as unyielding as an iceberg.

The only feminine discourse came from Bomber on the floor of the backseat, howling at the indignity of enforced imprisonment. When the cat's howls grew louder and too nerve-racking to ignore, Dante turned the CD player's volume up. The incomparable trumpet of Miles Davis blared through the speakers until Nicole reached forward and snapped off the music without asking.

"If you don't mind," she said. "I've got a screaming headache right now."

Yeah, right. A little cool jazz exacerbated her pain, but the cat's yowls were a symphony of tranquility. Scrambling for something to drown out the feline noise, he jerked his head at the green Jag ahead of them on the highway.

"Is that guy always such a jerk?"

Nicole whirled, eyes blazing. "Jason is married to my best friend. He's one of the nicest, most decent guys I know. So I'd appreciate it if you didn't call him a jerk, thank you very much."

"Okay, I'm sorry," he told her, though he had no clue what he was apologizing for.

The guy *had* acted like a jerk, from the cutoff at the stop sign to the nonsense about Nicole being in his bedroom. Still, the jerk had obviously helped Nicole out of some kind of trouble. So maybe he should cut the guy—and Nicole—a little slack. He had to constantly remind himself: Nicole was nothing like Linda. It wasn't fair to judge her based on another woman's history.

"What happened after I dropped you off?"

"Nothing," she mumbled.

"Obviously something happened."

"I don't want to talk about it."

"Why not? Isn't that why you're driving with me instead of with that— with your friend's husband?"

"No. I'm driving with you because Jason's a big boy who won't take offense if I don't ride with him. Unlike you who burst into the middle of something you didn't understand and proceeded to hurl insults without provocation." Slapping her hands in her lap, she glared at him with enough ice to freeze his blood. "Why did you come back?"

"What?"

"We'd said good-bye. You had to get back to Gitan, re-member? Didn't want to leave the kid alone for too long. So what made you come back to my house this afternoon?"

"I'd called the shop, and Gitan was fine." He shrugged. His actions made perfect sense to him. Why was she so bent out of shape? "I headed back to take you up on your invita-tion for a drink. I even stopped to pick up a bottle of wine. It's at your feet there."

He jerked his head to the brown paper bag tucked between the console and her seat. She spared it a scant glance then turned toward the window again.

"Twenty minutes too late," she muttered. "Story of my life."

"Why? What did I miss?"

She sighed. "Never mind."

"What happened in those twenty minutes?"

"Nothing."

"Don't say nothing," he said. "When I dropped you off, you were fine. When I come back less than a half hour later, you're bawling your eyes out and a Jaguar-driving, snot-talking idiot who thinks he's the next Jerry Seinfeld—"

"Leave Jason out of this."

"Yeah, yeah, I know. He's your white knight."

"I was upset and he came to get me. Besides, what busi-ness is it of yours? It's not like we're dating or anything."

"If we were, your white knight would be in traction at this minute."

"Do me a favor, Dante," she said flatly. "Drop me off and

go home. Go check on Gitan. Leave me—and my friends—alone."

The rest of the drive passed in uneasy silence until Dante followed the Jaguar up a long curving drive and through the wrought-iron gates of a Spanish hacienda-style estate. On the front steps, a pretty, dark-haired woman waited, hands clasped, worry etched on her face. He barely had the car in Park before Nicole flung open the door and raced up the stairs to the woman.

By the time Dante unbuckled his seat belt and stepped out of the car, both females had disappeared inside the house. He was left standing in the circular drive with Sir Jason.

The Jaguar's trunk popped up and Jason grabbed the two suitcases. "Scotch?"

"Huh?"

"Scotch. It's an alcoholic beverage, best served on the rocks in a crystal tumbler. You see, when one gentleman offers another a scotch, the offeree normally nods and says thank you. Then the two retire to a den or some other cozy room for a civilized conversation. I have no idea what Neanderthals do. Besides grunt."

"Oh, well, Neanderthals don't usually drink scotch before the sun's gone down."

"Then you're a stronger man than I," Jason replied with a wide grin. "Farrah gets me so worked up some days I could start looking for the scotch bottle at nine in the morning. Normally I resist, of course. But this is a special occasion. It's not often I get a guy here who's just as crazed over Nicole as I am over my wife."

"Thanks anyway, but I think I'll head home from here. Soon as I get that singing cat out of my backseat."

Jason's grin stretched to idiotic proportions. "Nicole told you to go home, didn't she? Made it sound more like 'Get lost' when she said it, I'll bet."

Lucky guess.

"It really doesn't matter if she said it or not," Dante insisted.

"Right. Because you don't care about her."

Impatience rippled the hair on his arms. "Who *are* you? Oprah?"

"Nope. Just a friend."

"I've got enough friends, thanks."

"Friends with insight into what's up with Nicole? 'Cuz I only know one person in this whole county who knows Nicole better than she knows herself. And that's my wife."

"Forget the psychobabble, okay? Why don't you bring the luggage inside and let me go home?"

"Because I recognize that confused look on your face. Three years ago, I wore it. And Nicole helped me figure out what made Farrah tick. I'm offering you the same help. Take it or leave it. But if you're smart, you'll save yourself a lot of time and sleepless nights by taking it."

"Thanks, but I've got more pressing things to deal with right now."

He returned to his car to retrieve the cat carrier, set it beside the bags at Jason's feet, and raced out of the insane asylum before whatever mental illness ran rampant there caught him in its grip.

Inside a beautifully decorated guest bedroom on the second floor, Nicole paced the polished oaken floors, hands clenched in tight fists. Her sneakers made little *squick-squeak* noises each time she pivoted on her toes. Even the fiery sunset, all pink and orange froth melding into the blue-gray line of the Long Island Sound, did nothing to calm her frazzled nerves. She only glanced out the French doors to the Juliet balcony in an effort to gauge the distance. Could she throw herself off that rail and end it all?

Not that she'd actually do it. She was simply speculating on the quickest end to her dilemma.

While calculating the possibility, she ticked off a list of insults. "Stubborn, arrogant, obnoxious . . ."

Seated cross-legged in a Queen Anne chair upholstered in burgundy cabbage roses, Farrah clucked. "Oh, come on, Nicole. This is nothing new. Your mother's always been—"

"Not my mother." Nicole stopped in midstride, her shoes releasing a squeak louder than an air brake. "Dante!"

Farrah's eyes widened, enhancing her doe features. "Oh. Right. Dante. I take it he was the guy in the blue Beemer?"

"No." Sarcasm dripped from her lips like poison honey. "My mother hired a car and driver to evict me. Of course that was him!"

Sinking onto the cherry sleigh bed, she scrubbed her hands over her face until her skin felt raw. Better her skin than her heart.

"I still can't believe it," she muttered. "Talk about perfect timing. If I hadn't come home when I did, she would have gotten away clean."

"Who?"

"My mother. Who else?" Nicole's head shot up, and she glared exasperation at Farrah. "Keep up here, will you?"

"Trust me, I'm trying," she replied, amusement animating her face. "Let's start over, okay? Tell me everything that happened today."

Hugging a crimson needlepoint throw pillow against her chest, she told her tale. In halting tones, she related the details of the canoeing adventure. She relived their disappointment at coming up with nothing even remotely useful in that day's treasure quest. She described Dante's chilly attitude and quick departure when he dropped her off and how she felt when she entered her house to find her mother conniving behind her back with that scrawny succubus-in-training, Kim Camilo. She explained her call to Jason, Dante's return, and ended with the ride here and her order to Dante to stay away from her and her friends.

When she finished her story, Farrah brushed a stray sable curl from her shoulder, but said nothing. Her big brown eyes shimmered with pity, an emotion Nicole despised.

"Well?" Her prompt erupted in a frustrated shout. "Say something."

Farrah simply shrugged. "What would you like me to say? You've had a pretty busy day. Give me a chance to digest it all, okay?"

The silence continued, with Farrah studying Nicole as if she were a specimen on a microscope slide. Under such intense scrutiny, Nicole squirmed. Drawing her knees up to her chest, she skooched against the headboard to make herself smaller. The longer Farrah remained mute, the more uncomfortable Nicole became. Her skin prickled. The fine hairs on her nape danced with static electricity. She could actually hear her heart thrumming behind her eardrums. And her headache returned with a vengeance, thumping against her skull in a heavy-metal rhythm.

When she could no longer bear the quiet, she blurted, "You wanna hear something weird?"

Farrah's brows shot up. "How weird?"

"Well, not ax-murderer weird," she retorted. "Just . . . I don't know . . . strange."

"Shoot."

"Okay, the other day I was at work, right? And this woman comes in. I'd shown her a bunch of places last week, but her husband's one of those 'the grout lines in the bathroom are uneven,' 'the high hats in the kitchen need to be upgraded' kinda guys. I spent four hours with them and walked away at the end of the day no closer to a sale than before they came in. I even showed them that townhouse in Seascape Villas."

"Yeah, and . . . ?"

"And he didn't like it last week because it was too big. But the wife came back this week because now all of a sudden she wants it. Seems she just found out she's pregnant and thinks one of the townhouse's bedrooms would make the perfect nursery."

"So? That's a good thing, isn't it? You're about to break your slump."

She hugged the pillow tighter. "Promise me you won't think I've lost it. This is gonna sound so totally bizarro."

"Come on, Nic. You know me better than that. Tell me already."

One sharp inhale for inner strength and she let it spill. "When I walked into the townhouse the other day, I was all set to sell it to the Shanahans. I mean, I was completely fired up, thinking this could be it, you know? The sale that breaks my slump. And then, all of a sudden, it was like someone pulled back a curtain and let the sun shine on my brain. I saw how dismal I'd let my life become, living in my mother's mausoleum. There was this moment of clarity where I pictured how different things could be if I let go of the fantasy and grabbed reality." She shook her head. "I'm mucking this up."

Farrah smiled. "No. I understand exactly what you mean. What did you do when you had this epiphany?"

Looking away from her best friend's expressive face, she stared out at the darkening sky. "I rushed poor Mrs. Shanahan out of there before she could fall in love with the place. Then, when we got back to my office, I practically pushed her to go home." She gave a bitter laugh. "I even told her to look at other homes and discuss all the pros and cons with her husband. Make sure the place was the perfect home for them."

"Because you want it for yourself?" Farrah suggested, her tone maternal.

Nicole shot out an index finger. "Congratulations. You've finally caught up."

"Well, thank God. I mean, it's about time you moved out of your mother's house. I'm glad you came to your senses. So did you put a binder on it? Tie it up in the meantime in case Mrs. Shanahan decides she wants it?"

Biting her lip, she shook her head.

"No? Why not?"

With anyone else, embarrassment would prevent her from disclosing the truth. But Farrah knew her better than anyone else. They'd shared tons of embarrassing moments during their long friendship: from school-age transgressions like cutting each other's hair to dating disasters like Farrah's panty-wearing pal, all the way into their adult lives. Farrah would never judge her harshly.

"I was looking for a sign," she admitted on a rush of exhaled air.

Sure enough, Farrah simply giggled her reply. "I'd say you got one. In big, blazing neon."

"I guess so." Mind made up, she pulled up the covers and snuggled beneath their warmth, cocooned for sleep. "Right now, though, I'm beat. I'm so not used to canoeing up and down rivers all day. And you should go downstairs and spend some time with your husband. Tomorrow I'll go to work early and talk to Natasha about—" She stopped short. "Oh, shoot."

"What now?"

"Dante still has my car. I said I'd walk to work for the rest of the week, but I can't do that from here."

A perfectly sculpted eyebrow rose in Nicole's direction. "Then you'll have to talk to him and get it back, won't you?"

Her cheeks simmered and she folded her arms over her

chest. "I have nothing to say to him right now. You should have heard him on the way here. For some weird reason, he took an instant dislike to Jason."

"Understandable," Farrah replied dismissively. "Jason can sometimes rub people the wrong way. Especially when he's trying to get a rise out of you at the same time. If Dante took Jason's teasing to heart—"

"Don't you dare take his side," Nicole snapped. "He's arrogant and stubborn—"

"And obnoxious," Farrah added with a smirk. "I know. I heard all those insults before. But from the glimpse I got on the front steps earlier, he's also tall, dark, and handsome. And he obviously cares about you. So those qualities far outweigh his detriments, in my opinion."

"Reserve your opinion until you've spoken with him. I'll bet Jason will give you an earful later." Hope burned anew. "Hey! Do you think Jason could drive me to work this week?"

Farrah's smirk broadened. "Nope."

"Aw, c'mon!"

Her slender shoulders rose and fell in a noncommittal shrug. "You want to get to work to buy that townhouse, you'll have to see Dante again first. Or at least talk to him."

"Thanks a lot," Nicole grumbled.

"Someday you'll say those words and mean them." Rising, Farrah reached to pick up the telephone handset from the bedside table. "In the meantime, you've got a phone call to make. I'll give you some privacy."

She strode to the door and disappeared on her final say. "Good luck!"

Chapter Seventeen

Dante made it back to the shop in record time. After zipping into his parking space, he climbed out of the car and strode into the garage.

"Dude!" Gitan greeted him. "Check it out." With a flourish, he gestured to the Honda, now gunmetal gray on all sides, blue tape framing every piece of glass or chrome.

Good God. Wasn't Reynaldo supposed to keep the kid from going overboard? Where was the old man anyway?

"I thought you were only going to repaint the passenger door."

"We thought about it," Gitan said. "But the paint job's so old we decided to do the whole car. Make it match better. What's Nicole's favorite color?"

"How would I know?"

"All *right*!" Gitan rolled his eyes in the manner of all

ticked-off teens. "It was just a question. You don't have to bite my head off. What happened? You two have a fight or something?"

"None of your business."

The kid had the guts to smile. "I'd say that's a big yes."

"Wipe that smirk off your face," Dante grumbled. "Where's Reynaldo?"

"Upstairs."

Dante headed in that direction, pausing only to toss over his shoulder, "Get your gear together."

"Why?" Gitan called after him. "We're not leaving yet, are we? I figured I'd get started on the sound system while the primer's drying."

He stopped. "Who said you could mess with her sound system?"

"You did. I told you I wanted to maybe get her new speakers."

"The operative word being maybe. Where did you get the speakers from anyway?"

"I stole 'em," he snapped. "Where do ya think I got 'em? I bought them."

"Where'd you get the money?"

"Oh, didn't I tell you? I sell drugs in my school now."

Dante's muscles clenched from the jaw down. "You know, I've had enough smart-aleck remarks for one day. Now get your gear together so we can go home."

Snapping his black boot heels together, Gitan gave a stiff salute. "Yes, sir!"

Suddenly, everyone was a comedian.

He scaled the steps to the office where he found Reynaldo on the phone. "Yeah, hold on," Reynaldo said to the caller. "I'll get him."

He pressed the red button to put the caller on hold, and then hit the intercom. "Gitan, pick up line two."

Once the red light stopped blinking, he turned to Dante. "Hey. How'd it go?"

"Don't ask." He sank into his chair, leaned back, then nodded at the telephone. "Who's on the phone?"

Reynaldo grinned. "Your girlfriend."

He jolted upright as if snapped from a rubber band. "Nicole?"

"Yeah. She sounds angry. You two have a fight or something?"

"Son of a—" Shooting to his feet, he pushed Reynaldo out of the way and picked up the phone, simultaneously pounding down the button for the second line. "Why are you calling Gitan?"

Nicole didn't miss a beat. "Why, I'm fine, thanks for asking, Dante."

"I know you're fine. I left you in the care of your wonderful friends, remember?"

"Yes, I know. Jason said you left skid marks on the paving stones when you peeled out."

The picture of Nicole and that Jason character laughing at him didn't sit well. "Answer my question. What do you want with my son?"

"Dude," Gitan cut in. "Take it easy. She just wanted to know about her car."

His anger deflated, and he pulled the chair behind his collapsing knees. What was wrong with him? He was reacting like a jealous husband. And Nicole didn't deserve that level of animosity. They were friends. Weren't they?

"I was gonna ask you about your favorite color," Gitan said to Nicole, drawing him back to their phone conversation.

"Why?" she asked.

"We need to repaint the whole car," he replied. "So if there's a special color you want, we could do it for you. Free of charge."

"Now, hold up, Gitan," he said, forcing a calm demeanor. If he didn't get ahold of this kid's tongue, he'd find himself signing over the company to her.

"Actually," she cut in, "I wanted to ask if I could come pick up the car tonight. Something's come up and I can't leave it after all."

"Umm . . ." Apparently, Gitan's extensive vocabulary had abandoned him.

Which meant Dante would have to deliver the bad news. "I'm sorry, Nicole," he said, smooth as Irish cream, "but the car's not drivable right now."

"Oh." A flat, unemotional syllable. And far from the temper tantrum he expected from the Nicole he'd left behind. "Okay. I guess I'll have to work something else out."

"We could lend you a car," Gitan offered. "The dude's got a bunch of 'em."

"Sure," Dante heard himself say. "Absolutely. Which one would you like?"

What choice did he have? Since she'd been kind enough to

accept when he'd begged her to do this for Gitan, he now had to provide her with some kind of car to offset her inconvenience.

"No, that's okay. It's my mess. I'll find a way out of it somehow. Good night."

Click.

Dante stared at the receiver, seeking answers. What mess? What exactly had happened this afternoon?

"Nicole?" Gitan called into the line. "You still there?"

"She hung up," Dante told him.

"She did? How come?"

"Why don't we go find out?" Dante turned to Reynaldo. "Feel like taking a detour with us before you go home?"

"Yeah, sure," Reynaldo replied. "What's up?"

"We're gonna drop the Acura off with Nicole so she's got a car until hers is finished."

Maybe take Jason up on his offer to talk to Farrah.

"All right!" Gitan exclaimed, still on the phone.

When Dante reached the fortress this time, the wrought-iron gates were firmly locked. At the beginning of the driveway, a call box prompted him to hit the Send button for entrance.

"Yes?" a woman's voice came through the speaker.

"I'm Dante LaPalma. I was hoping to see Nicole."

"Just a minute."

A mere second later, the gates slowly swung open.

"Cooooool!" Gitan enthused from the passenger seat.

"Yeah," Dante grumbled. "Neat-o."

He drove inside, waving Reynaldo to follow closely behind.

The way his luck had run so far that night, the gates would swing shut on the Acura, damaging the pristine paint and the resale value. Pulling to a stop in front of the redbrick walkway that led to the front door, he parked. He climbed out and waited for Reynaldo and Gitan, and then led the way up the rounded staircase to the front door.

Before he hit the landing, the door swung open. The same pretty woman he'd seen here earlier greeted them. "Mr. La-Palma." Her smile was warm, friendly, engaging. "Nicole's asleep."

"Oh."

Stupid. Now what should he do? He really hadn't expected Nicole to go to bed within thirty minutes of her phone call. "I just wanted to leave her a car to use until hers is ready. If you'd be kind enough to give her the keys, we won't bother you."

"Actually, if you have some time, I'd like to talk to you," she said, opening the door wider. "I'm Farrah Harriman. Please, come inside."

She ushered them into the expansive house as if welcoming old friends, and then turned to Gitan. "You must be Gitan. Nicole's told me about you."

"Yeah? What'd she say?"

"That you had excellent taste in music and a solid head on your shoulders."

"No sh—" One quick glance with eyebrow raised from Farrah had Gitan blushing as he censored himself. "No . . . kidding?"

Great. The kid was in love. Again. Not that Dante could blame him. Farrah Harriman exuded such sweetness, the most bitter heart would lose its bite. She also knew just the right thing to say to put a guest at ease. She was soft in her speech and mannerisms, and the direct polar opposite of her abrasive, wisecracking husband. Go figure.

"No kidding," she said to Gitan. "You know, we have a wonderful game room." She laughed. "I'm afraid my husband loves his toys. Would you like to see it?"

"Hel— er, heck, yeah!"

"Then follow me."

She led them through a long hallway, decorated with oil portraits, no doubt of various Harriman ancestors. They all wore the same look of cool disdain Dante had noted on Jason's face.

As she descended a flight of circular stairs, she whispered to Dante, "We'll be able to talk quietly here and you can keep an eye on Gitan from a safe distance."

"And your husband?" he asked, senses on full alert.

The guy was probably waiting around a corner in a suit of armor to pop out and startle them. Bozo.

Her smile lit her pretty face to angelic. "Jason's handling some business in his office. Overseas calls will keep him occupied for about an hour. Does that make you feel better?"

"Yeah," he admitted. Too late he considered censoring himself.

Oddly, she took no offense—at least not on the outside. "I thought so."

At the bottom of the staircase, she paused at an arched doorway, flipped on a series of lights, and welcomed them into a child's dream world. Pinball machines blinked and dinged red and white lights in one corner. A surround-sound theater system, complete with movie-style seats and mounted game controllers, took up the longest wall. An old-fashioned popcorn machine advertised FRESH HOT BUTTERED GOODNESS. The center of the room held several gaming tables: pool, foosball, air hockey, and poker, to name a few. There was a dartboard, a jukebox, and a dozen shelves filled top to bottom with board games.

"This is awesome!" Gitan announced in one heavy breath as he spun slowly, drinking it all in.

"Make yourself at home," Farrah said.

"Thanks!" He turned to Reynaldo. "Come on. I'll kick your butt in air hockey."

Once they were happily ensconced in the game, Farrah turned to Dante and nodded to a fully stocked bar in the farthest area of the gaming room. "Can I get you something to drink?"

"No, thanks. I'd better not. I'm driving." And he hadn't eaten since lunch. Alcohol didn't sit well on an empty stomach.

"Soda then?"

He picked up the vibe she'd be hurt if he didn't accept some form of hospitality. "Water would be good, if you've got it. But don't go to any trouble . . ."

"Of course. Sit, please." She led him to the bar, pointed at a stool on one side while she glided around behind the gleaming counter. She bent down, opened a small refrigerator, and pulled out a bottle of spring water, then placed it before him and waited.

Sensing she wouldn't relax until he'd accepted her offer, he unscrewed the cap and took a long swig. When he placed the bottle down again, her smile returned.

"First," she said, "let me apologize for my husband. Jason spent the first half of his life living for the wrong reasons. He now wants to make up for everything he missed." As if in explanation, she gestured around the game room. "He told me what occurred between the three of you this afternoon, and I'm sorry his teasing offended you. He really did it more to make Nicole squirm. Yet I get the feeling his intentions backfired."

"No apology necessary," he assured her.

He liked her. A lot. She was so genuine, so completely without guile, Ebenezer Scrooge wouldn't humbug Farrah Harriman.

"Ooh! You got *pwned*!" Gitan shouted from across the room.

Dante turned to see the kid doing a mini victory dance, apparently having just beaten Reynaldo in air hockey. Facing Farrah again, he jerked his head in Gitan's direction. "I don't suppose you want to take *this* kid off my hands."

"Only if you're willing to take Nicole off mine," she replied with a giggle.

"No, I think I got the easier task right now. So, tell me." He leaned cupped hands across the bar. "What did I miss today?"

Farrah's smile grew wistful. "Let's go back to the beginning first. Do you know how long I've known Nicole?"

"She said you've been best friends since you were kids."

"Kindergarten. It was mid-October. I used to stay after school every day. Wash the blackboards, put the chairs on top of the desks, collect any papers the other students left behind."

Sighing, she added, "Yes, I was one of *those* kids. Anyway, I was always the last one to leave, and after school I'd walk home. This particular day I saw a little girl sitting on the see-saw out on the playground. I knew something was up. The buses had left much earlier, and really, no kid besides me ever stayed at school that late. When I got closer, I could tell she was crying. I asked her what was wrong. She told me she didn't have a daddy anymore."

Sympathy and unease, twin snakes, coiled in Dante's belly. He remembered what Nicole had told him about the day she learned her father had left.

"I didn't fully understand what that meant, but I knew she was devastated. So I offered to share my daddy with her. I took her home with me and told my parents what she'd told me." She shrugged. "That was it. We were inseparable from that day on. My parents were great about including Nicole in everything we did. Vacations, slumber parties, weekends, Nicole was as much a part of our family as any of us."

She placed her hands flat on the bar, her expression serious. "And then her mother married Papa Joe when Nicole was seven. He was your grandfather, right?"

"Yeah."

"He was such a good man. We were all so happy for Nicole. Papa Joe doted on her, and she bloomed. Really. They were inseparable. Oh, she and I still hung out, but not every day anymore because Papa Joe took her everywhere with him. Ballgames, bike rides, movies, amusement parks, beaches. Sometimes I got to go too. In a sidecar on his motorcycle. As Gitan would say, 'It was awesome.'"

"I'll bet." Only another rider could understand the freedom of a motorcycle.

"Then one day I got home after school and there she was, curled up in my father's lap, bawling her lungs out." She ran a fingertip under each lower lid. "And I knew." The last word came out on a shaky breath, and she quickly busied herself with the glasses on a shelf behind her.

"You knew?"

She turned to look at him and sniffed to no avail. Caught in the high-hat lighting, a single tear glistened on its journey down her cheek. "I knew Papa Joe was gone. After that, well . . . Nicole never let another of her mother's husbands get close to her. She's carried that hurt over into her adult life, keeping men at a safe distance, never letting a tryst become serious. Her one solid relationship is with that house."

"The house she wants to buy from her mother."

Farrah's lips compressed in a tight line, and she nodded. "Until today."

His brain buzzed on overload, and he shook his head to clear it. "What exactly did I miss today?"

"When you dropped Nicole off this afternoon," Farrah said, "her mother was inside with a realtor. Apparently, some heated words were exchanged, and at the end of it all, Nicole announced she no longer wanted the house and would move out immediately. She called me because she had no place else to go. I was still at work so Jason sped over to the house."

Smiling, she lowered her voice to a whisper. "Rhoda's scared to death of Jason. Once Nicole mentioned Jason was coming to pick her up, Mom and the realtor hightailed it out of there so fast, they left a cloud of dust behind. Jason got there a few minutes later, helped her pack a few things, and . . ." She spread her hands wide. "You know the rest. He brought her here. And here's where she'll stay."

"Unless," a familiar namby-pamby voice said from the doorway, "you'd like to lend us some assistance."

Chapter Eighteen

Jason relaxed against the entryway as if he owned the joint. Which, in fact, he did. Still, despite Dante's fondness for the idiot's wife, something about Mr. Jaguar grated on his last nerve. Until the idiot stepped into the room.

Only a blind fool could miss the sparks flying between Farrah and Jason Harriman when they were near each other.

"All well in Brussels?" she asked her husband.

The sadness Dante had seen in her eyes when they'd discussed Nicole faded to sentimental longing.

"All is perfect in Brussels," Jason replied as he brushed a tendril from her cheek and kissed away the tear. "And you two? Did you fill him in on what he needed to know?"

"Most of it."

Slipping a possessive arm around Farrah, Jason said, "Dante. Nice to see you again."

And suddenly, Dante felt like the world's biggest moron. No way this guy had eyes for anyone but his wife. He owed Jason Harriman an apology. And Nicole, as well.

"Jason." To save face, he jerked a nod at the far wall. "Nice setup you got here."

"Your son seems to like it."

Turning, Dante spotted Gitan, now sitting in one of the movie seats, headphones in place, engrossed in some ATV racing game with Reynaldo. "I should probably take him home. He hasn't even had dinner yet—"

"Not a problem," Jason said. "We can call for a pizza or two. Gitan likes pizza, doesn't he?"

"He did last time he visited me," Dante admitted. "Now I have no idea what he likes."

"Being difficult, huh?" Farrah asked.

"To put it mildly," Dante replied.

"It's the age," she said. "He's . . . what? Fifteen? Sixteen?"

"Fifteen. And sometimes he acts like a forty-year-old; sometimes he's like nine. I can't blame him though. He has . . . issues he has to work out right now."

"Nothing a little pizza can't help with," Farrah said and slipped out of Jason's embrace. "I'll go see what kinds of toppings he wants and place an order. You two have a preference?"

"No anchovies," Jason said. "Anything else is fine. And while you take care of the pesky details, Dante and I will finally have that scotch. Something tells me if he isn't ready to drink yet, he will be very soon."

Running a cotton candy fingernail around his cleft chin,

Farrah cooed, "Poor baby. With both me and Nicole in the house I'm surprised you held out this long."

He clutched her wrist and kissed each fingertip slowly. "It's a testament to my manhood."

"Ahem!" Dante cleared his throat. These two could set the room on fire.

Rather than show embarrassment, Farrah simply flashed him another ethereal smile. "Sorry. Pizza coming up."

She strode to where Gitan sat, leaning one way then the other in the direction of his ATV on the television screen. With a grand bow, she pushed a button on the console and the images on-screen froze.

"Hey! What the—" The kid cut himself short when he saw Farrah, but not quick enough for Dante.

"Watch it, Gitan," he growled.

Jason laughed. "Relax. Farrah's used to getting the same reaction from me when she pulls that maneuver."

"Still," Dante replied, eyes shooting lasers at the kid. "It's disrespectful. Especially when she's been so generous."

"Sorry," a red-faced Gitan mumbled.

"We're ordering pizza for dinner," Farrah said in reply. "Interested?"

"Yeah, sure. Can we get pepperoni and sausage?"

"You can get anything but anchovies," she said with a wink in Jason's direction.

After flashing a thumbs-up, Jason reached beneath the bar, came up with a bottle, and set it on the bar with a musical thunk. The gold-and-black label spoke volumes to Dante. Imported and mucho expensive.

"A little nectar of the gods?" Jason pulled two tumblers off a shelf, added ice from the nearby bucket, and splashed the amber liquid into the glasses. Finished, he slid one to Dante, lifted the other, sipped, and swallowed. "Aaah. Now I can look at life through new eyes."

Raising his tumbler in mock salute, Dante followed suit. The moment the liquid slid down his throat he easily understood why Jason had pushed to drink earlier. Never in his life had he tasted anything so smooth, so rich, so perfectly balanced.

The room grew silent. Farrah had disappeared, Reynaldo and Gitan were buried in their game, headphones firmly in place, and Dante had no clue what to say to Jason.

Finally he settled on a good old-fashioned apology. "Sorry to barge in on you," he said. "If I'd known Nicole was asleep—"

"Forget it." Jason waved a hand, the one without the tumbler. "She was pretty wound up, even before she spoke to you. But afterward?" He winced. "Afterward, she was like that old Tasmanian Devil cartoon. Farrah talked her down, and she pretty much collapsed after that. Emotionally drained is how Farrah described it. Says she'll probably sleep 'til tomorrow." Jason tilted his glass. "So you and she are involved in some kind of treasure hunt?"

The scotch reversed direction in Dante's intestines. That was an odd non sequitur, and while he couldn't explain why, discomfort niggled into his stomach. For now, he'd play this game, but as close to the vest as possible.

"It's a requirement of my grandfather's will."

"What's in this game for you?"

He arched a brow at the man across the bar. Mr. Genial Host had reverted to Mr. Obnoxious. "Excuse me?"

"No offense, Dante. You see, Nicole was going along with this hunt in the hope she'd get enough money to buy off her mother. Fat chance, and I think she's finally realized that. But she's moving forward for your sake. Told Farrah you're in it for some noble cause. 'Noble,'" he reiterated. "That ups my curiosity."

Noble? She thought his adopting Gitan was noble?

Dante shook his head. "If you ask me, my cause is more selfish than noble."

No lie. He simply couldn't bear to lose his son, blood or not.

"Want a second opinion?"

He cast a meaningful glance at Gitan still engrossed in his video game with Reynaldo. "Can't."

"Ah." Jason nodded. "Got it. Say no more."

Somehow Dante doubted it. The details were too bizarre for anyone to grasp. Even he had trouble believing his life these days.

Truth is often stranger than fiction.

Jason tilted his empty tumbler in Dante's direction, clinking the cubes against the glass. "You know, while you've got the chance, you might want to confide in Farrah. She might be able to help."

Not unless she could convince Linda to see reason.

Dante drained the last of his scotch and felt the warmth blanket his jumpy insides into calming down. "Farrah wouldn't happen to run a travel agency, would she?"

"No." Jason pursed his lips. "But I have a contact I use pretty often for business who can cut you a great deal. Why? What do you need?"

He couldn't believe he was about to utter the words aloud, but they flew from his mouth of their own accord. "A first-class Hawaiian honeymoon."

Jason didn't even blink. "One week or two?"

Unable to sleep, Nicole picked up her purse and pulled out the last clue for yet another study session. By now the paper was dog-eared, with a brown ring in the center from an errant coffee cup, and a definite imprint on Nicole's brain. She barely needed to glance at the words anymore, except to study them for something she may have missed the first thousand times.

Seated at the cherry writing desk, she spread the paper smooth with the flat of her hand. "Okay, old man, what were you thinking when you wrote this?"

Sometimes you can't ride the wave to shore,
And you wind up beneath the sea.
But if you find something new that was old before,
Let the wave cast her spell, and she'll set you free.
A treasure awaits for the fun and the sport.
At last when the storm comes, you'll be cozy in port.

If canoeing on the Carmans River wasn't the right task, what else would fit this bizarre poem?

Ride the wave to shore . . .

Where else would she find waves?

Hell-o? A million and one places. From the Sound to the Atlantic Ocean to the Great South Bay, Long Island was surrounded by water.

Moving on. Next line.

You wind up beneath the sea.

Nothing to add there. She decided to skip down toward the bottom.

Let the wave cast her spell, and she'll set you free . . .

Who? Who would set them free? And why did they need to be set free? Free from what?

"Aaaaargh!" She growled her frustration in one loud roar and tilted her head toward the ceiling. "What makes you think we need to be free and cozy in some port?"

Wait a sec. Hold up. Free and cozy in port. Free in port. Cozy in port. Cozy port. Free port.

"Freeport!"

Excitement tingled her skin, and she shot up, reaching for the terrycloth robe Farrah had left for her on the Queen Anne chair. When she slipped it on, the white wrap enveloped her from neck to toes in fluff. Pushing open the French doors, she stepped out onto the tiny balcony. Cool terracotta tiles tickled her feet. A salty breeze kissed her cheeks and danced over her lips. The sound of water splashing against rocks whispered in her ears. Starlight twinkled on the Sound, as if some denizens of the sea winked a secret code meant just for her.

Freeport. That had to be what Papa Joe's poem meant. No pirates, but the Nautical Mile sat smack-dab in the middle of the South Shore town. She hadn't visited the area in years. But she still remembered that long stretch of road with restaurants and gift shops lining one side, a canal full of boats on the other. A tourist would be hard-pressed to find fresher seafood on Long Island. Each late afternoon, fishermen docked their vessels and simply strolled across the street with the day's catch.

Working with Freeport in mind, she forced her brain to consider the rest of the poem.

Sometimes you can't ride the wave to shore.

The surfing they'd done at Ditch Plains? Maybe.

And you wind up beneath the sea.

Okay, what was beneath the sea? Gripping the wrought-iron railing, she leaned forward, scanning the horizon spread out below.

Rocks. Lots of them. She still sported a few fabulous bruises on her hips and thighs from her surfing lessons and her many underwater foul-ups that day. What else lay beneath the sea?

Seaweed. Kelp. Sand. Buried treasure, of course. Did Papa Joe expect them to scuba dive for their treasure? Possible. But after today's disastrous escapade, she'd wait until she had more proof before running to Dante with a new scenario.

What was the next line? Something about finding something new that was old before. Too ambiguous. Could point to anything from the photos that had sent her down the Carmans River to a Broadway play revival. Moving on . . .

Let the wave cast her spell, and she'll set you free.

Nothing about diving or treasure there. But . . . wait! The next line: *A treasure awaits for the fun and the sport.*

Scuba diving's supposed to be fun. And she guessed it could technically be called a sport. Or was it more of a hobby? Something vacationers did in warm blue waters? Definitely not something done near the Nautical Mile.

Another dead end.

She inhaled sharply, forcing her memory backward. The first activity she and Dante shared came from her long ago days with Papa Joe. Although since she'd been a child at the time, she'd never jumped from a plane prior to her adventure with Dante. But she used to wait in the office of Drop Zone, week after week with her fudge bars, while the adults took part in the excitement.

Their second task, surfing, she'd never attempted before that afternoon at Ditch Plains. But Dante had. Papa Joe had taught him. So whatever the next requirement entailed, she assumed would be an activity one or both of them had shared with Papa Joe in the past.

Time to make the call.

With a quick glance at the clock, she picked up the telephone again: 8:45 P.M. Too late for Dante to still be at work. But she didn't have his home number.

She'd have to try his cell. At worst, she'd leave a message and hope he got back to her fairly quickly.

To her surprise, he picked up on the first ring. "Hello?"

His mellifluous voice flowed through her veins like heady wine.

"Ummm . . . hi." Brilliant. She sounded like a mental patient.

"Nicole?"

"Yeah." Moving the receiver away from her mouth, she coughed softly to regain her equilibrium. On a deep inhale, she added, "I'm sorry to bother you, but I've been playing around with that last clue again—"

"Hold that thought," he interrupted, but she cut off his brewing argument.

"I know I screwed up last time, but I think I might be on to something this time."

"Yeah, but—"

"Just listen first." She cut him off again. "Then you can discount what I say, okay?"

"Okay."

The amusement in his tone set her teeth on edge, but she ignored the feeling. Maybe once he heard what she had to say, he might not find her so comical.

"Did Papa Joe ever take you scuba diving?"

"No," he replied thoughtfully. "Why?"

The wave of excitement she'd been riding curled, crushing her in disappointment. "Forget it." She sighed. "I guess I was wrong. Again."

"Giving up that easy?" he replied. "Come on. You sounded pretty excited a minute ago. Maybe you should join us and we can all brainstorm a little. Between the six of us, we might come to the right conclusion."

"Six of you?" Automatically, she looked at the receiver in her hand. Yeah, right. Like some video screen would pop up and show her who he was with.

"Come on down," he said with the enthusiasm of that old game-show announcer.

"I can't. I'm not home right now, remember? I'm at Farrah's. And I'm currently without wheels, thanks to Gitan. Not that I'm pointing fingers or anything," she added quickly.

"Actually," he replied, "I'm closer than you think. You won't need wheels."

"Why? Where are you?"

"Downstairs in Jason's game room."

She nearly dropped the phone. "What are you doing here?"

"Gitan, Reynaldo, and I stopped by to drop off a car for you. Farrah said you were asleep so we came down to play a few games. We're about to eat if you'd like to join us. Farrah's ordered a pizza and—"

"Pizza?" Her stomach growled, reminding her she'd had nothing to eat since the chicken at lunch. "From Alberto's?"

Oh please, oh please, oh please . . .

Alberto's, the best pizza in the world, was a treat she didn't get often.

"I guess," he replied. "I didn't ask." From far away, she heard him ask, "Did Farrah order from Alberto's?"

Jason's shout reverberated through her earpiece. "Of course! Come on, Nic. If you don't hustle, the ends will be gone before you get here."

The ends, or corners of the square pie, were the best pieces.

"I'll be right down."

Chapter Nineteen

W hen Nicole left her room, voices and laughter rang up
from below and across the long hallway. Following the noise,
as well as the heady aromas of garlic and tomato sauce, she
scurried downstairs to find a crowd in the dining area. Gitan
sat beside a middle-aged, dark-haired man in a blue work shirt
with *Ironman Motor Works* scripted over the breast pocket.
Farrah, the consummate hostess, flitted around the brass and
glass octagon table, filling plastic cups with soda. Wonder of
wonders, Dante sat catty corner to Jason, the two talking in
hushed—yet civil—tones.

Two open boxes reigned over the center of the table. The
first held a pizza dotted with slices of sausage and pepperoni,
the second was covered with a mélange of sliced vegetables:
onions, red and yellow peppers, zucchini, broccoli, and mush-
rooms.

Dante must have sensed her presence because he looked up, locking dark, unfathomable eyes on hers. A smile softened his features, and Nicole's knees went watery.

"Hey," he murmured.

Her heart sped up as if he'd just fallen to his knees and declared undying love.

"There's my other little girl!"

Her focus swerved to the older man leaning in the doorway. "Mr. M!"

Roger Mitchell, Farrah's widower father, beamed as he opened up his arms. "Come on. Give me a hug."

Nicole didn't hesitate. Mr. M had been her saving grace throughout her childhood, the one constant male she could count on to never let her down. The minute she stepped into his embrace, he squeezed her tight. Love flowed through her for this special man who'd treated her like a second daughter from the moment they'd first met.

Drawing back, he studied her attire with crinkled eyes. "Aren't you girls a little old for slumber parties at this stage?"

"Nicole moved out of the beach house," Farrah announced. "She's staying here for a while until she can find another place to live."

Mr. M's smile disappeared. "Need I ask if your mother had anything to do with this sudden turn of events?"

"No," Nicole said firmly. "This was *my* decision. And I have my eye on a place I really think I can call home."

Mr. M squeezed her shoulder. "Then I'd say congratulations are in order." He jerked his chin at Dante who sat staring dubiously at the square of Alberto's pizza gracing his plate.

"That's the grandson?" he whispered.

She nodded and pulled him toward the table. "Mr. M, this is Dante LaPalma. Dante, meet Farrah's father, Mr. Mitchell."

Without attempting to mask his interest, Mr. M scanned Dante from head to toe. "He's got the look of his grandfather. Around the face. Big chip on his shoulder, though. He must have just met Jason."

"Daddy!" Farrah slapped a palm on the tabletop.

But Jason burst out in raucous laughter. "Actually we met this afternoon, but it's taking longer than usual for him to warm up to me."

"Did you offer him money?" Mr. M retorted.

"Better. I offered to help him arrange a Hawaiian honeymoon."

Nicole's lungs suddenly stopped working. "A . . ." She swallowed hard, thoughts of eating pizza replaced by the vision of her heart on a plate, a fork piercing its center. "A honeymoon?"

"Who's getting married now?" Gitan chimed in, gaze swerving from his father to her and back again.

"Your mother," Dante replied.

"Oh, right," the boy said, biting into his slice with gusto.

Nicole didn't share Gitan's placid reaction. In fact, she couldn't disguise her surprise. "You're paying for your exwife's honeymoon?"

Dante shrugged. "Trust me. There's a method to my madness."

"Well, he's got integrity," Mr. M cut in. "You gotta give him that much."

Farrah chose that moment to use her hostess powers. "Nicole, sit. Grab a slice."

"Yeah," Jason added. "I saved you an end."

Even Gitan attempted to change the subject. Patting the seat next to him, he called, "Sit here, Nicole. I saved you a place. You gotta try this stuff. It's totally awesome. They put the cheese on the bottom and the sauce on top. It's like totally upside down."

"Yes, I know," she said, forcing the tension from her shoulders.

"Lots of meat too," Gitan continued. "Not like in the place near us. You need a magnifying glass to see *their* toppings."

Jason laughed again. "No need to convince Nicole. She'd crawl across a carpet of thumbtacks for a slice of Alberto's."

Farrah held a paper plate out toward her father, who stood outside the circle of diners. "Have a slice, Daddy?"

He waved her off. "God, no. Not with my reflux. I'll be up all night."

"Sorry," she said, lowering the plate. "I forgot."

"I ate with the boys earlier, anyway." One hand rose to cover a yawn. "I think I'll just head upstairs and read for a while before bed. Good night, all."

As the diners paused long enough in their gastronomic joy to wish Mr. M good night, he strode away. Pausing in the doorway, he tossed over his shoulder, "Dante, Nicole. Good luck with your treasure hunt. Joe's counting on you to make him proud."

* * *

Caught in midswallow, Dante choked. No wonder the pizza was made upside down. This house was like some bizarre hall of mirrors at a carnival. Nothing was as it appeared.

Seated nearby, Nicole looked like a little girl, hair pulled up in a high ponytail, wearing a yellow T-shirt and monkey pajama bottoms. But her wide-eyed expression was anything but childlike as she called after the old man, "Mr. M, wait! What do you know about the treasure hunt?"

"Figure it out, Nicki," he replied, never turning around. "You're a smart girl."

He began to whistle while he strode away, the tune becoming less and less distinct as he disappeared into some distant corner of the house.

Dante shot a glance her way, but she turned her focus to Farrah, who watched them both with a secret smile playing about her lips.

"What do *you* know about the treasure?" Nicole asked.

Farrah laughed. "Almost nothing."

"Bull." Dante studied her carefully, watching for a telltale sign she wasn't being one hundred percent honest.

If not for the presence of so many outsiders—Gitan, Reynaldo, Jason—he would have fired questions until Farrah broke down and told them every secret in her closet.

But she never blinked under his intensity. "I swear I don't know anything. I mean, Nicole told me about Papa Joe's will, but as to any details . . ." She shrugged. "I'm just as much in the dark as you two."

"What about your father?" he pressed. "He obviously knows something."

"Yeah, well," Nicole muttered. "He would."

"Huh?" His gaze swerved to her. "What do you mean?"

Farrah leaned forward, her wide doe eyes pinning accusations on Nicole. "You didn't tell him?"

Nicole shook her head.

"Tell me what?" Dante demanded.

"Yeah," Gitan interjected. "What are we missing here? Are you really looking for treasure? Can I help?"

Reaching across the table, Farrah flipped the lid open on the pizza box. "Why don't you guys eat up while I take Dante and Nicole for a walk? Dante hasn't seen the rest of the house yet."

"Umm . . . actually, I'd prefer to stay here." Nicole bit into her slice, chewed, and then swallowed.

With her eyes closed and a long, delicious sigh escaping from her smiling lips, she lit up the room with her joy. When she opened her eyes again, they sparkled like Caribbean water beneath a brilliant sun.

He was falling for her. The realization struck like a wrecking ball to his chest. He should have struggled harder against the attraction. Even now, he expected more of a fight from his logical side at admitting his growing fondness for her. After all, the last thing he needed right now was the distraction of a "thing" with Nicole. But, like everything else that had happened since the meeting in the attorney's office, what he needed and what he got spanned more miles than the continental United States.

"I'm going to fill him in on *everything*, Nic." Farrah's thinly veiled hint drew him back into the conversation. "You sure you don't want to come along? In case you want to clarify anything I say?"

Dante watched the two women communicate through gestures. Farrah's eyes widened and she craned her neck forward while Nicole replied with a rapid head shake and a hand wave.

"Go," Nicole said at last. "I've had enough of my mother's machinations for one day."

Farrah sighed. "Okay." She took Dante by the hand. "Come on. Let me show you the rest of the house."

She led the way through an arched doorway and toward a room with walls of sand-colored marble. White leather furnishings and tables lent the room an austere aura.

"I call this the operating room," she said and shivered. "It's way too cold in here for my taste. But then I grew up with wall-to-wall shag carpeting and plastic on the furniture."

Despite his confusion, Dante smiled. Farrah Harriman was so genuine, so self-effacing, he wondered if anyone could ever harbor a grudge against her. No surprise she and Nicole were such close friends. The two women seemed to have a lot in common, including their down-to-earth attitudes. Nicole, however, had a sassy sense of humor that gave her the edge on his affection meter. Good thing, since he wouldn't want to get into a bidding war with Farrah's husband over her heart.

Apparently oblivious to his thoughts—thank God—she continued on past a series of closed doors, cataloging for his benefit: bathroom, office, her father's bedroom, yadda yadda yadda. She finally stopped outside another arched doorway. Right arm outstretched, she invited him inside. "This is my favorite room in the house."

He immediately knew why. The far wall was made up entirely of glass. This section of the house jutted out over the bluffs. Below them lay the rocky shoreline of the Long Island Sound. At this time of night, he couldn't see much more than the line where the water met the land and, in the distance, yellow lights from other homes set into other bluffs.

He imagined sunsets here would be a meld of strawberry daiquiri sky and foamy margarita sea. "Nice view."

"Thanks," she said and gestured to a large wicker loveseat with tropical cushions thicker than his bed's mattress. "Please. Make yourself comfortable."

He sank into the loveseat.

She took a chair opposite him, her long, golden legs folded Indian-style and her hands in her lap. "I told you how I found out about Papa Joe's departure, right?"

"You said you saw Nicole sitting with your father, crying, and you knew."

"Well, that's how *I* found out. But my dad, he knew before Nicole did. Papa Joe came to see him about a week earlier."

"Why?"

"Rhoda—Nicole's mother—she's a real piece of work. She never had any qualms about using Nicole as a pawn in her divorce negotiations. It started with her first husband and continued on down the line until Nicole turned eighteen and was no longer a viable weapon. I'm not sure what Rhoda held over Joe, but he had to promise to have no contact with Nicole ever again. He agreed, but only to get away clean. He never had any intention of keeping that promise."

The thought of anyone daring to separate a young girl from the father figure who loved her would normally leave a bad taste in his mouth. Knowing both characters in this scenario, however, upped distaste to outright disgust.

Farrah's steady gaze fixed on his face, and a flush crept up his neck.

"So my grandfather used your father to keep tabs on her," he summed up.

Her teeth caught her lower lip, and she nodded. "Daddy made sure Joe got school photos, vacation snapshots, prom pictures. They had phone conversations every week. My father kept Joe informed of every milestone, even after Nicole started her own correspondence with him."

"How long did all this last?"

"Right up until Joe passed away."

"So your father knows about the treasure hunt?"

A stray tress of hair fell before her eyes, and she blew it back with a puff of exhaled air. "He not only knows about the hunt, but what the treasure is at the end."

He stiffened. Was it possible?

"No way. In his video to us, Gramps said the attorney was the only one who knew all the details."

"Believe what you want." When the curl fell before her face again, she gathered her hair in one fist and tucked it inside her collar. "I've always thought of Papa Joe as someone who covered all his bases. But maybe I'm wrong."

She had a point.

"Okay, say I believe you. Where is this treasure?"

"I already told you, I don't know anything more than what

Nicole's confided so far. I have my suspicions, of course, but when I told Nicole, she laughed at me."

"What are your suspicions then?"

She held up a hand. "No thanks. I'll take ridicule from Nic because she's my best friend. But I don't think I'd like to have you scoff at me."

"What makes you think I'd scoff?"

Her laughter tinkled across the room, and the flush on his neck heated to volcanic temperatures.

"No offense, Dante, but so far you haven't exactly given me the warm and fuzzies since I met you. And I'm not sharing my romantic nature with a man who is liable to belittle me in my own home."

He didn't know whether to argue with her mistake regarding his character or pursue her confession regarding hers. He opted for the former. "I would never—"

"Get the chance if Jason was in the room," she finished. "So let's just drop the subject, shall we?"

"Not until I get a chance to talk to your father again."

She shook her head. "No dice, Dante. Whatever my father knows, he won't tell until you've covered whatever Joe planned for you. Daddy's no soft touch, which is probably why Joe trusted him with the details. I should imagine if you cheat or try to cut corners, your inheritance will become null and void."

Which meant he should rejoin Nicole in the dining room to see what she'd come up with on their latest clue. And suddenly, spending time with Nicole, whether jumping from planes or cleaning out a garbage scow, didn't seem like such a hardship.

Chapter Twenty

After Gitan devoured his fourth slice of pizza, he challenged Reynaldo to another round of air hockey in the game room. Grateful for the reprieve so the adults might talk, Dante waved them off. Once Gitan and Reynaldo fled the room, he glanced around at the three others remaining.

"Let's brainstorm, kids." He turned to Nicole. "What were you saying earlier about scuba diving?"

"It was a theory." She recited the poem again for Jason and Farrah's benefit. "I'm thinking the bit about being free in port points to Freeport. And with all the water references, I'd narrow it down to the Nautical Mile."

Farrah, whisking empty plates and cups from the table, paused, and then nodded. "I can see that. It makes sense—in a twisted Papa Joe kind of way."

"Except there's no scuba diving in Freeport," Jason said.

"At least," Dante added, "not Freeport, New York. Freeport in the Bahamas, yes."

"Oh, God," Nicole exclaimed, her face pale and eyes wide with panic. "You don't think we're expected to go to the Bahamas, do you?"

Dante shook his head.

"But how can you be sure?" Farrah asked.

"The Yankees," Dante replied.

"Huh?" Jason blinked rapidly.

"I'm with Jason," Nicole said. "You'll have to explain that one."

"All the references to the Yankees in our original letters? We never did find a link for that. And I think it means we're supposed to stay in New York to find our treasure."

"What makes you say that?"

He shrugged as if he didn't care, but pride laced his words nonetheless. "I've been doing a little research of my own. The one commonality we missed when we considered Lou Gehrig and Joe DiMaggio? Both men only played major-league ball for the New York Yankees. Babe Ruth played in Boston. And rumor has it, one year the Yanks tried to trade Gehrig to the Sox to make up for them losing the Babe, but Boston passed on the deal."

Nicole slapped her forehead with a palm. "Oh my God, how stupid am I?"

Stupid? No. Adorable? Yes. Especially when her lower lip disappeared behind her teeth whenever she grew frustrated.

"Don't sell yourself short," he said. "You're three for four so far on the Joe Corbet Circuit. I just happened to get lucky. Once."

"What made you think about scuba diving, Nicole?" Jason asked.

"The line about winding up beneath the sea. I started thinking about what you find underwater. Seaweed, rocks, treasure . . ."

"Fish," Dante added, almost as an afterthought.

All motion in the room stopped.

"Fish." The way she said the simple term, with wonder in her tone and a slow shake of her head, suggested she hadn't thought of ocean life when first running through her list.

"Of course!" Farrah exclaimed. "And there are plenty of party fishing boats on the Nautical Mile."

"Did your grandfather take you fishing?"

"Sure. You?"

"All the time."

"Well, Dante"—Jason clapped a hand on his shoulder— "I'd say you just went two for two on the Joe Corbet Circuit."

"We'll need a list of available party boats," Nicole said.

"I'll check online," Jason said and flipped a BlackBerry out of his pocket.

While Jason punched information into the device, Dante kept his gaze pinned to Nicole. She must have felt the heat in his eyes, because her cheeks flamed rosy red, and she squirmed in her chair. She had a tiny speck of tomato sauce on the corner of her lip. If they were alone at this very minute, he'd kiss that speck away and revel in the taste of her mouth, the smooth column of her neck . . .

"Got it," Jason exclaimed—not a moment too soon. "The current list of party boats available for rental are the *Annie J*, the *Argo*, the *Bonnie Lass*, *Cracker Jack*, the *Dolphin*, *Driftwood*, the *Emerald*, *Flying Clipper*, *High Tide*, *Jolly Roger*, *Liberty Belle*—"

"Wait!" Nicole cut him off. "Go back. What was that Clipper one?"

"*Flying Clipper*? Run by Captain Lou Ridley."

The key words clicked in Dante's brain at the same time that realization lit up Nicole's face. Clipper and Lou. Again.

"Bingo."

"Let's be careful," Nicole warned. "Jason, go through the rest of the list. Make sure nothing else jumps out at us."

He read through them all, from *Mama's Boy* to *Yellowtail*, but none of the names resonated with the same gotcha feeling as the *Flying Clipper*.

"That has to be it," Nicole said.

"Okay, so how soon can you take the day off for a fishing expedition?"

"Not 'til next Thursday," she said on a sigh.

"Fear not," Jason interjected. "They have night fishing."

Dante and Nicole shared a smile.

"So, Nicole," Farrah said brightly. "Take off tomorrow to clean your stuff out of your mother's house during the day and go fishing with Dante tomorrow night. It's a perfect plan."

Yes. This felt right. And even if they came up empty-handed again, Dante found himself looking forward to another adventure with Nicole. "I'll make a reservation."

*   *   *

No pangs of guilt stabbed Nicole when she called in sick to work the next day. Because she'd told no lie when she informed her boss she felt like the walking dead. Her head swam in swamp water, dark and murky. Her eyes refused to remain open, much less focus. And every muscle in her body required twice as much energy as normal to move.

She never should have asked Farrah for those sleep aids. But after Farrah recited the plans already set in motion for her for the next day, Nicole had been too wound up to even think of sleeping.

Now she'd pay for her oblivion with a foggy brain and feet mired in quicksand.

After stumbling into a pair of jean capris and a powder blue lacy tank top, she headed downstairs and found Jason seated in the breakfast nook, smearing raspberry preserves on an English muffin.

"Want one?" he asked.

As if expecting her to turn him down, her stomach growled noisily.

Grinning, Jason handed her his muffin. "Here. I'll make myself another." He rose to tend to a new breakfast for himself, and she greedily bit into the crispy toast.

While the second muffin toasted to a golden brown, Jason turned, thermal carafe in hand. "Coffee?"

"Need you ask?"

Jason returned to the table, a mug of steaming coffee for her, a second English muffin for himself. "What's on your agenda today?"

"Packing, I guess," she said on a sigh. "I'll have to rent a storage unit and a moving truck."

"Farrah left a number for you. Tony Marinello can lend you his truck and two of his gorillas for the day."

"Great." She didn't even attempt to hide the acid in her tone. Tony Marinello, a good friend of Farrah's, owned a construction company. Which meant she'd called him sometime last night while Nicole was zonked on those magic blue pills. "She might've asked me before making any arrangements."

Jason shot his monogrammed cuffs, inspected a minuscule stray thread, and frowned. "You know her. She doesn't want you to second-guess your decision to leave."

Figured. Lucky Farrah, always so obsessed with doing the right thing.

"God," she exclaimed, "how do you stand being married to someone so perfect?"

"I wouldn't know. You'll have to ask Farrah when she gets home."

She nearly choked on the last bite.

At her sputtering, he waved a hand. "No wisecracks, please. You all set for today?"

"No."

"Oh, well, maybe when you see the car Dante left, you'll perk up."

"Really?" Excitement tingled her brain cells. "Why? What kind did he leave me?"

"Does it matter?"

Did it matter? Well, yeah. In plain language she wanted to believe he cared enough to send the very best. Like Hallmark. Still, she wouldn't show that kind of vulnerability to Jason.

"I'm just curious," she replied instead. "What kind of car is it?"

"What kind?" He paused for a moment, one hand holding a knife layered with raspberry preserves. "A blue one, I think. It's parked out front. If you've finished your breakfast, get out of here. You have work to do."

"What about you?"

"I'm working from home today."

"Let me guess," she said. "Your wife set you up to watchdog me so I don't change my mind. Right?"

"No. I've a golf game scheduled at Shinnecock for this afternoon and didn't feel like schlepping into the city only to turn around and come back again."

She studied him closely, and he never flinched under her scrutiny. His hazel-eyed gaze stayed focused somewhere between her forehead and her nose.

"Liar."

"Honestly." He rose, took their cups to the sink, and turned on the water. "But as long as I'm here, why don't you call Tony so I can tell Farrah you did?"

Shaking her head, she headed for the phone. As she passed him, she muttered, "I never thought I'd see the day where you voluntarily washed dishes."

He ran a dishcloth over the inside of a cup. "Love does strange things to a person."

Yeah, no kidding . . .

Chapter Twenty-one

Resentful but resigned, Nicole called Tony Marinello. He must have been waiting near the phone because he picked up on the first ring. Sure enough, he and two of his workers were ready to go. With no other choice, Nicole gave them the address and promised to be there as soon as she secured a storage unit and bought some empty packing boxes.

She purposely waited until she sat behind the wheel of the Acura before making her second call of the day. She'd fallen in love with the gleaming car the minute she saw it. Never before had she felt so regal. When she settled into the driver's seat, the black leather cradled her tush like a jewel nestled on velvet. The dashboard's wood burl highlights glistened under the sun streaming through the moonroof. The car came equipped with a GPS system, satellite radio, power everything, even heated seats, which she had no use for in August.

Eat your heart out, Cinderella. A girl could definitely get used to this kind of carriage. Inside her temporary luxury cocoon, she picked up her cell and dialed Dante's work number.

"Ironman Motor Works," he barked.

"Um . . . Dante? It's me. Nicole. I wanted to say thank you for the car. It's really more than I expected."

"You're welcome," he replied.

"Of course"—she giggled—"I'll never be satisfied with my little dinky Honda now."

"Yeah, well, your dinky Honda won't be so dinky once Gitan's done with it. The kid's bucking for an episode of *Pimp My Ride.*"

She fumbled with the phone, her hands growing sweaty. "What do you mean? I thought he was only giving me a paint job. Dante, please. Don't let him go overboard. I mean, they were just a bunch of CDs. I can't afford to pay for—"

"Forget it. Consider it a gift. You helped me with Gitan; we fixed your car. Even, right?"

Hardly. But what choice did she have? Better to change the subject. "Are we all set for fishing tonight?"

"You bet."

"I don't suppose good old Captain Lou gave you any information when you made the reservation?"

"Are you kidding? That would be way too easy. Somewhere above us, Gramps is enjoying the show we're providing him these days."

The thought made her smile. "Okay, well, I'll be at the house most of the day. Packing. If you need me, call my cell.

Knowing my mother, she's probably already changed the phone number at the house."

"Will do. I'll see you later, then."

"Dante?"

"Yeah?"

"Thanks again."

"No," he said firmly. "Thank you. One of these days, I'll explain why what you've done means so much. But for now, just know I appreciate it."

Before she could ask what that cryptic statement meant, he hung up.

Less than an hour later, Nicole arrived at what up until the night before had been her home. The minute she stepped inside she realized she needn't have gone through the trouble of securing the empty boxes. Apparently, while she had slept the sleep of the pill-swallowing unconscious, her mother had spent a fortune in overtime wages to have some stranger pack up her stuff. Two dozen boxes, emblazoned with the logo of a national moving company, formed a six-foot-tall blockade in the kitchen. Each box was neatly labeled with a thick black Sharpie in her mother's perfect handwriting: *Nicole's clothes, Nicole's dishes, Nicole's miscellaneous.*

Nicole's miscellaneous? What did that mean?

Struggling to take in the scene, she swallowed hard. The sleeping pills had made her fuzzy, but not so fuzzy she saw things that didn't exist. These boxes were real. And every single one of them was another brick in the Great Wall barricading her from any loving relationship with her mother.

"Hey, Nicole! Is this everything?"

She turned to see short, stocky Tony Marinello flanked by two heavily tattooed Yetis.

"Um, it's a start," she said slowly.

No need for everyone to know her mother couldn't wait to get rid of her. Telling Tony was like playing that old kids' game, telephone. Before long, the whole town would have a twisted variation of the truth.

"We'll get the dollies," Tony replied and jerked his head for Bigfoot One and Bigfoot Two to follow him out.

Once alone, she meandered around the boxes to get a look at the rest of the rooms. The only item still in the fridge was the lightbulb. Well, that and the annoying hum from the broken ice maker. No dishes sat in the cupboards. Mr. Coffee no longer waited on the counter to bring her caffeinated joy.

Why hadn't she ever noticed how shabby this room had become? The fruit and ivy vines in the wallpaper looked tired. The paper itself was filmy, marked by brighter squares where her photos and knickknacks once hung. The ceiling fan above her had pockmarks in the fake wood blades. Several cabinet doors sagged slightly on their hinges. Years of water damage had eaten the finish away from the doors below the sink.

Depression threatened to drown her in self-pity.

Get up, girl. Get out of this room.

Heeding her inner voice, she rose and walked into the living room. God, this room was even sadder than the kitchen. The old furniture remained, but no awning-striped curtains covered the windows. The late-morning sun shone like a spotlight on the emptiness. No colorful hand-crocheted afghan, a gift from Farrah's late mother, draped the couch. Bomber's scratching post, habitually in the corner to keep her from pulling up sections of the threadbare carpet with her claws, had vanished. The bookshelf, normally crammed with romance novels she'd collected over a twenty-year span, held nothing but dust. Ditto for her CD tower. The carpet was so stained scientists with spectrometers couldn't discern its original color. The cushions of the chairs and couch contained more lumps than pancake batter.

Her belly flip-flopping, she wandered down the hall. Forget the pink-and-black decor of the bathroom. She wouldn't even attempt to justify that 1960s sin in her mind. The good news? Rhoda had left the toilet paper on the spindle, a sliver of soap in the dish, and a lone towel on the bar. All personal products, right down to the citrus air freshener Nicole favored, had pulled the same disappearing act.

Which left her with the two bedrooms. Outside the door to her room, she paused, sucking in air as if about to be tossed into the deep end of a swimming pool. Her chest hurt, a thousand red-hot knives piercing her heart at once.

On a deep inhale, she pushed the door open. Her bedroom since infancy had been completely renovated a few years ago. Now, however, with all her furniture packed away, her drapes and mosquito netting removed, her beloved photographs boxed and out of sight, she noticed the imperfections her rose-colored glasses had prevented her from seeing all those years. The windows were too small and, despite her obsession with

Windex, didn't offer a clear view of anything. Even the sand appeared grainy, and not in a good way. A stifling stickiness cloaked the air. The white walls loomed like giant icebergs, surrounding her, encasing her like some extinct specimen trapped during the last Ice Age.

Unbidden, her thoughts turned to the townhouse in Seascape Villas. She pictured that sunny lemon bedroom with its wide windows, vaulted ceiling, and skylights. She saw the living room with the huge bay window. Like a film sped up, she watched the changing of the seasons through that window: cherry trees filled with pink blossoms in spring, the green grass and flitting dragonflies of summer, autumn's colorful leaves, and a white blanket of snow in winter, all in the blink of an eye.

Shaking herself from her stupor, she stepped into the hall, closing the door behind her. She didn't bother to cross the hall. The master bedroom lay unoccupied, untouched since her mother had moved out twelve years earlier.

Why hadn't she seen how hideous this place really was? Why had she fought so hard and for so long to keep it? For what? For fond memories of her childhood? True, the happiest moments of her life had been spent inside these walls. But the house didn't hold the memories she wanted to keep; her heart did.

Besides, there were just as many unpleasant memories attached to these rooms as nice ones. Her parents screaming at each other; nights spent alone and crying over Papa Joe's departure; endless arguments with her mother about clothes, hair, boys, college. Why in the world would she want to memorialize the site of so much pain?

She could hear a choir of angels singing, "Alleluia!" in her head. And she suddenly knew what she had to do. Something she should've done a long time ago. Or at least last week.

Leaving the house, she didn't look back, didn't feel any regret or misery. Once inside the borrowed Acura, she grabbed her cell. The battery was getting low; she'd have to charge it soon. But there was still enough juice for one more phone call. And she used that juice to call her office.

"Natasha?" she said after her boss answered with the usual spiel. "It's Nicole."

"Nicole, darling, how are you feeling?"

"Better, thanks. As a matter of fact, I'm on my way in."

"Really? But why? The office is only open for another hour. Why not stay home and rest a bit more? Come in refreshed and ready to sell your heart out tomorrow."

"I'm not coming in as an employee," she said, starting the car. "I'm coming in as a client."

Chapter Twenty-two

T rue to his word, Jason came through with an impressive Hawaiian honeymoon package at a cut-rate price. Five islands, all with oceanfront rooms, and prepaid tours for Diamond Head, the Pearl Harbor Memorial, and the Dole Pineapple Factory.

And Dante couldn't wait to forward the package to Linda. If it meant he'd gain full custody of Gitan, he would've included his heart on a stick.

After copying the pertinent paperwork, he stuffed the tickets and itineraries into a large envelope. In a separate file, he added a few of the legal forms regarding Gitan's possible adoption. He did not include the Termination of Parental Rights form, sensing the document's title could cause Linda to feel guilt, real or imagined, about something as final as "termination." By 9 A.M., he'd taken the entire packet to the post office for express mailing. Back at home again, he purposely waited until Gitan padded into the bathroom and slid the shower door into place before calling Linda to fill her in on the details.

"I must say, Dante, I'm impressed," she said when he'd finished his recitation. "This all sounds fabulous. You must really want something important to be so generous."

Despite knowing she enjoyed needling him, he felt his ire grow. "You know what I want. Can we bypass the games for now and get right to it? I'm pressed for time."

"Oh, all right." Linda sighed, her obvious need to toy with him overshadowing his exasperation. "So . . . Curt and I discussed your demand—"

"It's not a demand," he interjected. "It's a request. For Gitan's sake."

"Yeah, right." *Whoosh.* Her deep exhale of cigarette smoke whispered through the receiver. "I know what you mean. He'd be so much better off with someone not in any way related to him."

Nice. She still had enough acid in her mouth to disintegrate gold.

"I just don't want to continue shuttling him from Florida to New York. He needs stability."

"Oh, what? So now I'm a bad mother? Do you have any idea how difficult it is to raise a teenager alone?"

Here we go. True to form, Linda took his concerns about Gitan and twisted them into a conversation about her.

"I didn't say you're a bad mother, Linda." He kept his tone measured, calm, each syllable smooth as a new windshield. "In fact, I think you've done a great job with him. So now it's your turn. I figure this move would be good for all of you. For all of us. A clean cut so Gitan can get on with his life without feeling like a Ping-Pong ball."

"Well, to be honest, Curt seems to see things your way," Linda replied.

Figures. Based on what Gitan had said, the guy saw Gitan's permanent move to New York as a major partying opportunity. After all, Gitan might be Curt's son by blood, but there was no bond there. In fact, Gitan was closer to Dante in personality and interests than he'd ever been to Curt.

But he bit back the angry retort and settled for a more sedate, "So what do you think? Can we finalize this? For all our sakes?"

Whatever Linda said in reply was drowned out by the sudden slamming of the front door and subsequent house tremors.

Oh, God, no! Gitan should have still been in the shower. Had the kid overheard him on the phone? Alarm bells ringing, he replayed his side of the conversation through his mind. What Gitan heard: a move, a clean cut, a chance to get on with his life, spelled a misunderstanding of disastrous proportions.

"Linda, I gotta go," he said. "I'll call you later."

"Dante? What—?"

He hung up the phone and raced down the stairs to catch his son before all hell broke loose.

"You've reached Nicole at 555-6758. If this is Derek Jeter calling for a date, try my home phone, 555-8971. Everyone else . . . leave a message. Unless you're a friend of Derek's hoping to set us up. In that case the first rule applies. Thanks, and have a great day. *Beeeeeeeep!*"

Dante stuffed his cell into the case clipped to his belt with enough force to launch it into the earth's core. Why didn't she pick up her phone? He'd already left three messages on the cell, two on her home phone—despite the fact that he had nothing to do with Derek Jeter. Why didn't she call back already?

Like a skulking burglar, he patrolled the grounds of her mother's beach house, peering in windows, knocking on doors, to no avail. Where was she? She'd told him she planned to be at the house all day, but the place was totally empty. He'd hung around here for forty minutes—forty valuable minutes he could've been searching for Gitan.

No sign of her and no sign of Gitan, either. Not since ten this morning, when, according to Reynaldo, he'd popped up at the garage, face dark with fury. Without a word, he headed straight to Nicole's Honda, grabbed something out of the glove compartment, hastily stuffed it into his backpack, and then disappeared again. What had he taken? And where had he gone?

Dante had checked, albeit quietly, with all the kid's friends. He didn't dare let Gitan's disappearance reach Linda somehow. She'd skew the adoption before she had ever ascertained the facts.

Where should he search next? West toward the city? East toward the North Fork? The sun had gone from a brutal white spotlight to a quickly dimming ball of orange on the horizon. It would be dark soon. And Long Island was just too big for him to search by himself. But even if he wanted to involve the police in the search, he doubted they'd get involved. Gitan was nearly sixteen. Less than twenty-four hours had elapsed since the kid had stormed out of the house.

Only one other place he could turn.

Just before sunset, he pulled up outside the now-familiar wrought-iron gates. No sign of the Acura he'd lent to Nicole. Dante's heart twisted. Was it possible Gitan had pulled her phone number out of the Honda, she'd picked him up somewhere, and now was trying to talk him into going home? Not normally a religious man, Dante turned his eyes toward the BMW's moonroof and murmured a litany.

"Please let them be together. Please, please, please . . ."

Weird. A few weeks ago he wouldn't have let Nicole Fleming within missile-launching distance of his dog. If he'd had a dog. But over time, with all they'd undertaken and all he'd learned about her, he'd gained a lot of respect for her. And of all the people he knew, if Gitan ran from him to someone else, he prayed the kid had run to Nicole. Nicole, who knew a little about what Gitan might be feeling, would set him straight and keep him from doing something stupid.

Without warning, the gates squealed and slid apart, allowing him access. He took it as a good sign, some kind of signal from the Almighty, and drove onto the grounds with hope sparking a new flame inside him. The front door opened before he climbed out of the car. When he finally stood on weak-kneed legs, Jason bounded down the steps toward him.

"Well, well, look who's back. Can't get enough of us, eh?"

"Not now, Harriman," Dante said. "Where's Nicole?"

"She's at the beach house packing up."

When Jason's Cheshire cat expression turned to confusion, the flame in Dante flickered out like a blown-out birthday candle.

"No, she's not," he said. "I just came from there. I take it you haven't heard from her?"

"Not since she left this morning," Jason replied, "but I just got home a little while ago. Jeez, you look like hell. What's going on?"

Dante raked a hand through his hair. "Gitan's run away." Swallowing his pride, he croaked out, "I need your help."

Strangely, Jason didn't make a joke or scoff at the declaration. Instead, he suddenly became the cool head in the time of crisis. As if completely accustomed to frantic men who looked like hell showing up in his driveway begging for help. "You think he might be with Nicole?"

Hearing Jason utter the same idea reignited the flame for Dante. Desperate, he clung to that flicker of fire as if it were a lifeline. "God, I hope so."

Otherwise, he had no hope left.

Chapter Twenty-three

"Are you sure about this?"

Nicole stood in the foyer of the sunny townhouse and beamed at Natasha. "Absolutely."

Just like before, the walls in this place embraced and welcomed her. The memories of happy days with Papa Joe would always stay safely tucked away in her heart. But here, here was a place to make new memories, to create a future completely separate from the past and her mother. Yes . . . this was good. This was right. She should have made the move a long time ago.

"All right, then," Natasha said on a happy sigh. "You know the drill. I'll give you some time to wander around. When you're ready to return to the office, we'll complete the paperwork to put a binder on the place. After that, it's up to you to get a mortgage commitment. Think you'll have any problem with that?"

"Nope."

Thanks to years of scrimping, she had amassed a nice-sized chunk to put down as a deposit. Her local bank would no doubt be thrilled to tie her into a fifteen- or twenty-year commitment. With a nod, Natasha turned and left her alone to bond with her soon-to-be new home. Yep, this baby was as good as hers.

Wouldn't everyone be surprised? She really should call Farrah. Let her know what she'd chosen to do. Guaranteed, her friend's first reaction would be "Thank God."

Mind made up, Nicole dug into her purse to pull out her cell phone and found it deader than Elvis. Darn it! Her car charger was still in her Honda and Mom must have packed the AC charger with all her other "miscellaneous" items.

For now, she'd enjoy her first time in her new house. Strolling into the cheery living room, she envisioned where her photos would hang. Along the wall that separated this room from the dining room looked like the perfect spot. Lots of wide space, no glare from the expanse of windows. Of course, she'd need new furniture. Colonial or contemporary? Now that she thought about it, she'd always hated the heavy dark wood and plaid upholstery in the beach house. This room fairly screamed for cushy, overstuffed chairs and smoked-glass tables.

On to the kitchen. What color linens would best reflect the bluish tones of the bleached maple cabinetry? Purples, mauves, maybe a little gray. Her feet itched to dance on the slate tile floor. Decorating this place was going to be so much fun!

Upstairs, she headed for the master bedroom, but barely glanced at it. Her bedroom at the beach house had always been her oasis, and the same theme would work beautifully in here. Even more so, thanks to the giant skylights cut into the cathedral ceiling, which let in enough sun to dazzle, but would also allow for some gorgeous stargazing on clear nights.

In the master bath, she looked with longing at the step-in Jacuzzi large enough for two. Ooh, just the thought of reclining in a tub of turbulent water, easing the tension from sore muscles . . .

"Nicole?" Natasha's strident voice rang up from the foyer.

Pushing aside her decadent fantasies, she left the master bath and raced to the banister to see Natasha staring up from the first floor. "Something wrong?"

"There's a call for you on my cell. That nice Mr. Harriman. He says it's urgent."

Panic slammed her chest like a ninety-mile-an-hour fastball. Farrah. Oh, God, something had happened to Farrah. Why else would Jason go to such lengths to track her down?

"D-did he say what he wanted?"

Natasha held up the silver Motorola. "Ask him yourself. Chris gave him my number."

Not good. Seriously not good. Dread propelled her down the stairs with the speed of a turbo engine. She was still a few feet away when she dove past the last step and clutched at the phone Natasha held.

"Jason? What is it? What's wrong? Where's Farrah?" The questions came out in a breathless rush.

"She's fine." His tone was calm, but solemn. "She's here with me. So is Dante. It's Gitan. He's missing."

"I'm on my way." Without waiting for a reply, she slid the phone closed and flipped it into a shocked Natasha's hand. "Sorry. The paperwork's gotta wait."

Too anxious to sit, Dante paced the Harrimans' atrium. Good God, where was Gitan? Where was his son? He'd been gone for nearly nine hours now.

The intercom overhead buzzed, and Farrah rose. "That'll be Nicole."

"Stay with *him*," Jason said. "I'll get the gates."

Dante stopped pacing and watched Jason stride out of the room. His heart beat in staccato rhythm.

"We'll find him, Dante," Farrah's lyrical voice floated through his panic, attempting to placate, failing miserably. "Between the four of us, we'll figure it out."

God love her for trying. And how he prayed she was right! But he could barely breathe, barely think straight. Swallowing the lump that rose in his throat, he nodded.

Jason returned a few minutes later, Nicole in tow. "Dante, what happened? Tell me everything."

"No time for everything," Jason said. "He can fill you in as we go along. First, do you have any idea where the kid might have gone?"

"N-no. Why would I? I mean, I barely know him." She turned her angry gaze to Dante. "What set him off anyway?"

"A misunderstanding," he replied. "Reynaldo said he came by the garage and pulled something from your glove compartment, then took off. What could he want in your glove compartment?"

Blue eyes widened with innocence. "I swear, I don't know."

Another dead end.

Well, what did you expect? That she'd tell you he probably grabbed the tracking device she kept there for teenage runaways?

"Think, Nicole," Farrah urged. "What do you keep in the glove compartment?"

Nicole shrugged. "The usual. Road maps, a flashlight, the car charger for my cell, the owner's manual, my insurance card."

"Anything else?"

Lines etched her forehead, and he knew she was trying to picture the storage space in her mind. "I don't think so."

Jason nodded at Dante. "You think Reynaldo is still at the garage?"

"If he isn't, he's not too far. He lives three blocks away."

"Call him. See if he can take stock of what's in the glove compartment. If we have an idea what's missing, we might get a clue about where the kid went."

Why hadn't he thought of that himself? Because his brain was too frazzled maybe? Whatever the reason, he found a new respect for Jason Harriman.

From the moment Dante had fully apprised him of the situation, Jason had taken control. He'd filled in his father-in-law about Dante wanting to adopt Gitan, and Gitan misunderstanding what he'd overheard. Mr. Mitchell had immediately taken off to gather a posse of searchers from his Rotary Club.

Meanwhile, Jason e-mailed copies of the photo from Dante's wallet to dozens of different teen hangouts: fast-food joints, movie theaters, even a skate park, with clear instructions to simply call if Gitan showed up. He did the same with the local precinct, asking for confidentiality. The effort was a mere drop in the ocean of places Gitan might have run to, but gratitude washed over Dante that Jason would go to such lengths.

Now Dante dialed the garage and waited, praying Reynaldo had stuck around. Sure enough, the old man picked up on the fourth ring. "Dante?"

"Yeah. Any news?"

"I was kinda hoping you had news for me," Reynaldo said. "I haven't seen the kid since this morning."

Dante's heart plummeted and pooled at his feet.

"I figured I'd hang around here in case he came back, but so far, no such luck."

"I appreciate you thinking of it," Dante replied. "Listen, I want you to do me a favor. Go down to the Honda and open the glove compartment. Tell me everything that's in it. If there's so much as a gum wrapper wedged in the seams, I wanna know. Got it?"

"Yeah, sure. Hold on."

Half a dozen worried eyes watched him as he ticked off the time through the beating of his heart. One, two, three . . . He reached fifty-four before he heard Reynaldo fumble with the phone again. "Dante?"

"Yeah?"

"You ready?"

"Shoot."

"There's a big yellow flashlight, a coupla Atlas road maps, a dollar bill with 'Good luck' written over George's face, two Forever stamps, some kind of charger that plugs into the cigarette lighter, and the owner's manual."

"That's everything?"

"Yup."

"Okay, hold on." Quickly, Dante rattled off the list to Nicole. "Anything sound out of the ordinary?"

"No . . ." She stopped her head in midshake. "Wait! Yes. Ask him about my insurance card."

Dante did and received a negative. "You sure you had it there?"

"Absolutely. The only time I remove it is to replace the expired card every six months. It should be in a clear plastic sleeve with a zipper across the top."

Again, Dante relayed the info to Reynaldo and waited another few minutes for verification.

"No, boss. It ain't here. I even checked under the seats and atop the visors. No case, no card. You think that's what he took?"

"Maybe. You mind sticking around a little longer?"

"You kidding? I just ordered Chicken Delight delivery. I'm here for the long haul. Figure I'll put in some O.T. on the Cobra while I'm waiting to hear about the kid."

"Thanks, Reynaldo."

"No sweat, boss. Keep me posted."

"You got it."

Hanging up, he looked at Nicole. "No insurance card anywhere in the car."

"But that doesn't make sense," Farrah sputtered. "Why would he want your insurance card?"

Judging by the confused expressions facing him, none of them could figure out a logical reason.

"Did you have any money in that clear plastic sleeve?" he asked Nicole. "A credit card?"

"No," she insisted. "Nothing but the insurance card."

"So what could be so important about your insurance card to a sixteen-year-old?" Jason asked.

"Beats me." Nicole shrugged. "It's got the basics: VIN number, make, and model of the car . . ." The light of understanding clicked on in her bright eyes. "And my home address."

"I was already at your place," Dante said. "He wasn't there."

Nicole quirked a brow. "Where'd you look?"

"What do you mean?"

"I mean," she said on a humorless laugh, "that my house sits on a couple of acres of beachfront property. There are outbuildings galore down there. Cabana, boathouse, storage shed. Oodles of places for an angry kid to hide."

"If he was there, why wouldn't he come out when he saw me?"

"Probably because you're the one he's angry with. So I repeat, why don't you tell me what happened before he left?"

Dante sighed. Maybe she was right. If she knew all the facts she might understand why he bolted and where. "He overheard a telephone conversation between his mother and me. I think he got the wrong impression from what he heard. And he didn't wait for me to explain. He stormed out of the house before I could even hang up."

"Explain on the way," Jason interjected, shooing them with swept hands. "Go. Check the house and outbuildings. Farrah and I will stay here and coordinate things from this end."

Nicole nodded and then jerked her head at Dante. "Let's go. I'll drive."

"I'll drive, thanks."

"No, I'll drive. I know the shortcuts from here."

"You can give me directions."

She whirled on him, face drawn into tight lines. "If we're going under the assumption he's at my place and didn't make an appearance when you were there earlier because he's angry with you, I think it would be better if we let him think I've come home alone."

"Fine. Then I'll drive 'til we reach the intersection near the house, and then we'll switch places."

"That's the stupidest thing I've ever heard. What if he sees us?"

"Don't argue," Farrah cut in. "Just go!"

A flush of shame crept up Dante's neck. Who cared if Nicole wanted to drive? She had a valid point; Gitan might come out of hiding if he thought she was alone. But he was anxious to reach the kid, make sure he knew the truth. He shouldn't have kept the adoption a secret from Gitan. Imagine the pain he might have saved them both if he'd just been honest from the start.

"You drive," he said to Nicole in soft surrender.

"Go!" Farrah repeated.

Nicole sped out of the room, keys jangling from her fingertips. Dante paused, offered one last nod to the Harrimans. "Thanks. We'll call you."

"Will you go already?" Farrah exclaimed. "Time enough for thank-yous and sentiments when that boy is safe and sound."

He followed Nicole out of the house and down the front steps to the Acura.

"I hope you can handle this, 'cuz I'm done being dainty with the car," she announced as she yanked open the driver's door. "Buckle up and hold on!"

After clipping the seat belt into place he reached to close the passenger door, but she peeled out while he was still bent over. If he hadn't already clamped himself into place, the force would have flung him through the windshield. Fighting the wind, he managed to get the car door closed without injury.

Sccccrrrrrittttttccchhh! The undercarriage scraped the curb as the car left the driveway and met the street. He winced, but said nothing. Any damage to the car could be fixed. The Acura was metal and paint. Gitan was a thousand times more important than this box on wheels. Provided they made it there safely . . .

Nicole had driving skills that would make her a champ on the NASCAR circuit. The car hugged turns while she never eased up on the gas pedal. Traffic and storefronts whizzed by in blurs of color. The way she weaved through lanes, he might need a Dramamine before the ride was over.

"Talk," she ordered as she flung him against the passenger door with another tight turn. "What did Gitan overhear?"

"A conversation between my ex and me."

"You said that."

She ran a yellow light quickly changing to red, and somewhere to the left of him, a semi's airhorn blared displeasure. He gripped the dashboard hard enough to leave leather bits under his fingernails.

Maybe he *should* clear his conscience, make this his last confession in case his next destination was more final than he'd planned.

"I was talking to Linda about a permanent arrangement for Gitan," he said.

"What kind of 'permanent'?"

"A permanent legal arrangement."

Th-thunk! The car jumped the curb at the corner of her block; the same corner where Jason had pulled his illegal blow-the-stop-sign maneuver days earlier. Something dangerous about that particular intersection.

"You were going to let him go? Forever?" she demanded, taking her eyes off the road to focus all her anger on him.

The car veered onto the left side and he leaned over to straighten the wheel.

"Sorry," she mumbled and returned her attention to her wild driving. "But I'm furious. Why would you let him go?"

"I didn't," he insisted. "Though I'm assuming that's what he thinks too."

"So?"

"I want to adopt him."

She pulled into her driveway and slammed the gear shift into the P slot. The entire car shuddered at the impact. Turning off the engine, she twisted to face him across the center console. "You do? Really?"

Five simple words. That's all it had taken for him to go from villain to hero in Nicole's eyes.

"You know," she said, grabbing his hand and squeezing lightly, "when I first met you in that lawyer's office, I thought you were the most arrogant, cold man I'd ever come across. But . . . I was wrong. I think you're the most amazing person in the world. And I . . ." She coughed, looking at a space four inches to the right of his ear. "I think I really like you, maybe even love you. Is that weird? I mean, I know we haven't known each other very long . . ."

Wow. She had impeccable timing, didn't she? "Nicole, I—"

"Don't say anything." She cut him off with an upraised hand. "Especially not about how you like me but just as a friend or a sister or the nice lady who lives down the block, okay?"

"I wasn't going to say that," he assured her. "But I don't think now's the time to discuss our feelings for each other."

A rosy glow colored her cheeks. "Yeah, I know. I got carried away. It's been an enlightening few days for me." She turned from his scrutiny and opened the car door. "I'm gonna go up by myself. If I find Gitan, I want some time alone with him. To sort him out a little. Then I'll come and get you, okay?"

He might have argued. And if he hadn't been so shell-shocked from her little adoration speech, he definitely would have. But now, all he could do was nod, watch her walk away, and silently thank the ghost of a certain old man that they'd been thrown together.

Chapter Twenty-four

Nicole scaled the concrete stairs to the back door and shoved a key inside the lock. A few body slams later, she stumbled into the dark kitchen. "Gitan? Are you in here?"

She flipped lights on as she walked to the living room. No one. From living room to hallway. Empty. Down the hallway to the first bedroom. Zip. Second bedroom. Exactly as she'd left it. In fact, the entire house looked exactly as it had when she left that afternoon.

He must not have come into the house. Undaunted, she grabbed a battery-operated lantern from the utility cabinet and left the house. After locking the door, she strode to the planking that led down to the beach. Her feet thumped on the worn wood as she scanned both sides, lantern held high, throwing a tunnel of white light over the crystal sand.

"Gitan?"

A pair of seagulls screeched and took flight in reply to her call. The first building lay just ahead. The storage shed. But the door was still chained, and the rust coating the metal links and padlock didn't look smeared or disturbed in any way.

Moving on . . .

Another dozen yards away lay the boathouse. And oh, dear God, did she see a light in the window? Weak, a candle or flashlight maybe, but yes, definitely light coming from the boathouse. Leaving her lantern in the sand, she raced the rest of the way to the clapboard shack. Surely he'd heard her calling him. Yet he hadn't bothered to answer.

Well, if that's how he wanted to play, she'd go along with his game. Did he honestly think he could hide from her down here? She knew this place as well as she knew the house up-shore. She'd played in the boathouse for years, following her father around the cans of turpentine and marine paint. Papa Joe loved to tinker down there, had stored his Harley there, kept the photo of Tina Louise on the wall near the wide door used for moving boats in and out. And in later years, when she'd wanted to be totally alone, she would use the ladder hidden inside the false wall to climb to the top hatch a story above the main floor.

She headed there now, located the familiar rungs behind the shakes, and began her ascent. When she reached the top, she found the hook already open. So that was how Gitan got in too.

Quietly, she lifted the door and crawled inside, landing on the soft pile of old quilts placed there for her benefit twenty-five years earlier. They cushioned her fall and stifled any noise her older bones might have made. Once assured she'd survived the sojourn so far, she crawled to the edge of the balcony and peered down.

She spotted him instantly, seated cross-legged on the floor, dark head bowed over half a wilted submarine sandwich. An open bag of potato chips and a sweaty cardboard soft-drink cup waited beside him.

"Feel like splitting that?" she called and was rewarded with a look of surprise when he snapped his gaze to her perch.

"How'd you find me?"

She pointed to the flashlight sitting on its base in front of him. "I guess you didn't know this, but at night, that little gizmo shines around this beach better than the Fire Island Lighthouse."

"Oh," he said and bowed his head to the sandwich again.

She inched her way to the ladder leading downward and slung a leg over the rail. Gee, if she'd wanted this much of a workout, she'd have gone to the gym and tied herself to a Stair-Master.

By the time she reached the bottom, her legs shook like Jell-O. Maybe she should consider hitting that gym every once in a while. What was the sense in paying for a membership if she never used it? Putting the dues on her charge card every two years didn't exactly burn up the old calories, did it?

"On second thought," she said as she approached his picnic setup. "Skip the meal. I'll settle for a lettuce leaf and some water."

The kid didn't crack a smile. Great. This was going super well so far.

"Wanna tell me what you're doing here?" she asked and settled down across from him in the same cross-legged pose.

He shrugged. "I just had to get away for a while."

"Mmm," she replied. "I've always loved to come here and be by myself. Think. Dream of the day I'd be on my own and not have to answer to anybody but me. Is that why you're here?"

"I guess."

"Especially when my mother ticked me off. She'd say something stupid, or I'd misinterpret something she said and race down here, climb inside, and hang out 'til my anger cooled."

"I didn't misinterpret squat! My fath— the old man's trying to get rid of me."

She feigned ignorance. "Really? Why?"

"Because he doesn't want to 'continue shuttling me back and forth between here and Florida.' " The last bit of his statement was made while he screwed up his face and affected a deep, nasal twang somewhere between Kermit the Frog and James Earl Jones.

Still, she kept the innocent mask in place. "He told you that?"

"No, I heard him on the phone with my mother. He said he wanted a clean cut for *my benefit*. What a bunch of bull. He just wants me out of his life. After all, why would he want a kid who's not really his hanging around?"

"Because, blood or not, you're my son."

At the sound of his voice, Nicole's neck swung up to the overhang where sure enough, Dante squatted.

"You were supposed to wait in the car," she said, pointing a finger at him.

"You were taking too long," he replied.

Swinging over the rail, he took the ladder with the grace of a wild and exotic feline. On visits to the Bronx Zoo, she'd always loved the panthers. But, God, this man was sleeker and more appealing than any jungle cat.

"Gitan," he said as he slowly walked toward them. "You got it all wrong."

The teen shot to his feet. "Says you! I know what I heard. All that bull about a new life for Mom and Curt and a permanent break—"

"Yeah, but what you didn't hear was that I was trying to get you to live *here* permanently."

The words came out harsh and loud. So loud, Nicole could've sworn seagulls on the building's roof took off at the sound.

"Here," Dante repeated in a much softer tone. "With me. While your mother starts a new life in Florida with Curt. Gitan, I've asked your mother to let me adopt you."

Touched but uncomfortable at this emotional scene, Nicole rose and wandered around the boathouse, trying to give them some privacy. Still, she saw Gitan's expression was wary, a deer released by the big, bad hunter.

"I swear," Dante continued. "I don't want to send you back to Florida. I want you to stay here."

That's when Nicole spotted it: a giant black *X*, like those drawn on treasure maps, painted on the cupboard door where Tina Louise's photo used to hang.

Gitan picked up the nearby soft-drink cup and sucked the liquid dry. After shaking the last of the ice around the bottom, he started sliding the straw in and out of the plastic lid. The continual action made a squeaky scraping sound not unlike nails on a chalkboard. Dante winced, and not only because of the noise. Based on the sullen expression, the tightened lips and downcast eyes, he knew Gitan had his doubts about their discussion.

Jeez, how could he reach the kid? Convince him this wasn't a trick?

"The papers are all at home," Dante assured him. "Well, copies anyway. I mailed the originals to your mother this morning."

Gitan's head snapped up from the cup, one eyebrow arched. "No bull?"

"No bull."

The frown returned to curl his upper lip, almost a sneer. "Will she sign them?"

"That's what we were discussing when you took off this morning. I was trying to convince her this arrangement would benefit all of us. But she loves you so much she's in no hurry to let you go for good."

A total lie. Linda's hesitation had more to do with how much she could bilk out of Dante than any maternal love for Gitan. But the kid had been hurt enough by his parents' mistakes. No reason to make him hate his mother forever.

"So . . ." Gitan traced circles on the concrete floor with the moist tip of the soda straw. "What happens now?"

"Now? We wait. Hopefully, your mother will see things my way, and we can start making your visit here a permanent one. I'd like to have everything in order before school starts so I can get you registered."

"You serious?"

Ah, at last. A reaction he could appreciate. "Totally."

"For good, right? No probation where if I don't live up to your expectations in six months, you ship me back."

"For good. No strings attached." He pointed an accusatory finger. "But you've gotta talk to me, Gitan. Especially when you're angry. You can't go running out on me every time I say or do something that ticks you off." He forced a light-hearted grin. "Otherwise you may as well move in with Nicole now."

He jerked a head in her direction and found her staring at the other side of the boathouse.

Now what?

All thoughts of the reunion happening behind Nicole vanished as she simply stared at that black cross. She raised a fingertip to trace the outline of the glossy black paint: tacky. *Fresh.* Like, hours fresh.

"Gitan?" She turned to face the two males, pointing to the black *X.* "Did you do this?"

They paused in their deep conversation, gazed at the *X,* and then at her.

"No," Gitan said.

Eyes still fixed on where she pointed, Dante stepped toward her. "Are you saying that's new?"

She nodded. "The paint's still a little wet. Which means someone put it here within the last several hours."

"I'll bet it was that old guy," Gitan offered.

Dante swerved back to Gitan. "What old guy?"

Gitan sighed, slapped his hands at his sides. "See, after I heard you on the phone, I went to the garage. I dug out Nicole's insurance card from her car and caught a cab here. Which you obviously figured out."

He raked his gaze over both of them, eyes glinting with amusement but the typical teenager frown twisting his lips. "I got here late this morning, thought I'd talk to Nicole, you know? But she had all those moving men here, so I came down to the beach to wait them out. When I heard the truck leave, I walked back up to the house, but Nicole was gone too. So I started roaming around and I found this little house. I climbed up to that window there." He pointed to the site where both Nicole and Dante had recently entered the building.

"Is that when you saw the old guy?" Dante demanded.

"No. The place was empty so I hung out here for a little while. But it got really hot and I didn't want to open the windows in case someone spotted me in here. I decided to go down to the beach again, take a swim, cool off. When I came back, those big doors were open and the old guy was just climbing into a car and driving away."

Nicole's mind scrambled in a thousand different directions at warp speed. One of Papa Joe's friends? It had to be. But who? Someone she knew? And why now? What did it mean?

"Can you describe the old guy?"

"Yeah," Gitan replied. "It was the old guy from that big house the other night."

"Farrah's father?" Dante asked.

"Yeah."

Nicole paused, swallowed a lump of tears that rose up from her heart. "Mr. Mitchell was in the boathouse today?"

"Yeah."

"Well, now, that makes sense, doesn't it?" Dante said.

Nicole teetered on the edge of disbelief. "It does?"

He shrugged. "When we saw him last night, he mentioned the treasure. According to Farrah he knows all about it. Which means . . ." He strode to where she stood and placed a hand on the storage cabinet's knob. "The mysterious treasure we were supposed to find could very well lie behind this door."

Nicole's heart lurched. If whatever they sought lay inside that cabinet, their time together was about to come to an end. All the outings: skydiving, surfing, canoeing, the upcoming fishing trip, their late-night talks, everything would cease. And she'd be alone again. In a new house. Was it wrong to pray that the cabinet was empty?

Yes. She knew it was selfish. Just because her goals had changed and she no longer cared about a mysterious treasure didn't mean Dante didn't still need the money it might bring. In fact, he probably hoped to use whatever the treasure was to bribe his ex-wife into signing the adoption papers. How could she take that hope away from him? From Gitan?

But she didn't want their adventure to be over. The times she spent with Dante were the most exciting, happy moments she'd experienced since she'd lost Papa Joe all those years ago.

Dante twisted the knob, but Nicole quickly slapped a hand on the door to slam it shut again.

"Wait!" she said before she lost her nerve. It was now or never. "Before we open this, I need to ask you something."

"What?" He cocked his head in her direction, and Nicole had to squeeze her fingers into fists to keep from touching his face, his hair, the curve of his jaw.

Heat infused her from head to toe. *Come on, chicken. Get it over with.*

"I want to know how you feel about me."

"Now?"

"Yes, now."

Before we open the cabinet. So I can at least be fairly certain you're not lying to me.

Instead of stiffening, his posture relaxed. His smile grew lazy and he actually removed his hand from the cabinet door. "You," he said to Gitan over his shoulder. "Take a walk for a coupla minutes."

Gitan snorted. "You got it." He strolled to the wide doors, gripped the handle, and flung them wide. "Just remember. I'm within earshot, young and impressionable."

When Dante turned his attention back to her, Nicole looked away. On second thought, maybe she really didn't need to know about his feelings.

What if he couldn't wait to be rid of her?

Could her self-esteem handle the blow?

No way.

"You know what?" she said quickly. "Forget I said any-thing. That was stupid. Tell Gitan to come back; let's open this cabinet and see what's inside."

"Oh, no you don't," he exclaimed on a laugh. "You asked for this."

Yeah, she had. And she suddenly wished her mouth came equipped with rewind and erase buttons for instances like this.

"So," he said with an exaggerated sigh. "You want to know how I feel about you, huh?"

"No . . . yes . . . no." God, she sounded like a moron. "Look, this is stupid. Let's just open the cabinet—"

"Yours is the last face I see before I fall asleep," he said, leaning close.

So close his exhales tickled her cheek.

"Every day I know I'm going to see you is a good day no matter what else is happening. What does that tell you?"

"It tells me you watch too many Hugh Grant movies," she said with a flip of her hair. Secretly, though, a thrill danced inside her.

"That's not nice," he replied, his voice a husky growl that sent her dancing thrill shivering. "Here you put me on the spot, in front of my son no less, and then when I pour out my heart to you, you criticize my offering."

"So . . ." She stared at her feet, kicked an old rusted bolt ly-ing there. "Are you saying you might want to see me again, even after this treasure hunt is over?"

"That's what this is about? Oh, come on, Nicole. Look. Here it is in a nutshell. When I first met you, I was prepared to dislike you on sight. If for no other reason than because my grandfather adored you. And then you turned out to be pretty, which was another strike against you."

"Why?"

"Never mind why. All you need to know is that no matter how hard I tried, I couldn't dislike you. I fell for you from the moment I spotted that Band-Aid on your purple sandal. Treasure or no treasure, I want you in my life for as long as you can put up with me. How's that?"

Throwing her arms around his neck, she pulled him close. "An excellent start."

Chapter Twenty-five

"Mr. Stern will see you now."

At the receptionist's announcement Dante stood and took Nicole's hand. Together they walked into the conference room where they'd met nine months before.

The attorney rose from his seat at the head of the long table, hand extended. "Mr. LaPalma, Ms. Fleming, nice to see you again. Congratulations on your success. No doubt, old Joe Corbet's slapping St. Peter on the back and spouting 'I told you so' to every cherub who'll listen."

Dante couldn't stifle an amused snort. "He planned it all, didn't he? Right down to us becoming a couple." He shot a look at Nicole meant to make her melt.

Based on the way she sank into her chair, it worked. He smiled. It always did.

"I'd rather say he *hoped*, especially about the couple

263

part," Mr. Stern replied. "Your romance wasn't part of the legal arrangement. Even Joe Corbet didn't have that much power. Did you bring the key with you today?"

"Of course." Nicole fished through her purse for the key they'd found in the cabinet at the boathouse on that eventful evening last summer.

At today's meeting, rather than allow a table to separate them, Dante took the seat beside her. A clang sang in his ears as she grasped the old Harley Davidson emblem ring and dangled it before the attorney.

Mr. Stern clapped. "Excellent! If you'll just pass that over to me . . ." He took the key and lifted a small treasure chest from below the conference table.

Dante studied the old wooden chest, about the size of a child's lunch box, with rusted iron straps, and an old-fashioned padlock. "You're kidding, right?"

"No, I'm not. Your key will open this chest." With a wink, he inserted their key in the lock.

Beside him, Nicole sucked in her breath and held it.

The lock disengaged and Mr. Stern flipped the lid to remove . . .

A CD.

Déjà vu all over again.

The attorney popped the disc into the player and hit the button on his console. Sure enough, Papa Joe's face filled the television screen once more. This time, his grin looked wide enough to swallow his face.

"Congratulations, you two. You did it! I knew you would. By now, you probably know there is no money to be had."

Nicole took his hand and squeezed gently.

Yeah, they'd figured that out a while ago. But that didn't mean they wouldn't both be far richer before the end of the day. If all went according to plan, Nicole would accept Dante's marriage proposal later that night. She'd be sporting the engagement ring he currently cradled in his breast pocket. He'd finally have the perfect family with Gitan, his son, and Nicole, his wife.

Money, jewels, rare baseball cards—none of that mattered.

What did matter was their time together over the last several months. The airplane jumps, the surfing lessons, fishing trips, canoe rides, ski vacations, even simple walks on the beach were a treasure to be savored.

From the moment they'd found that key, he and Nicole hadn't spent a day apart. And he intended to keep seeing her until the day he died.

"Both of you needed to wake up." Papa Joe's voice crackled like crumpled waxed paper into his psyche. "And stop hiding from life. By now, you've learned what's important. Old Roger Mitchell wouldn't have let you have the key if you didn't deserve it. So Nicole finally got the gumption to leave that decrepit old house. And Dante finally woke up to realize that no matter whose blood runs through his veins, that boy is his by love.

"And speaking of love . . . how about you give my girl a kiss from her Papa Joe, eh, Dante?"

"Gladly," Dante told the screen and pulled Nicole into his embrace.

He kissed her wholly, soundly, and with enough passion to

7/09

wilt her. When the stars in her eyes finally faded, she
her gaze skyward.

"Thanks, Papa Joe," she murmured.

Somewhere above them, Dante swore he heard laug